MAGICALLY BONDED

HUNTED WITCH AGENCY - BOOK 2

Magically Bonded

Copyright © 2017 by Rachel Medhurst

ISBN: 978-1981939718

Published in 2017

This book is dedicated to Corinne

Other Books in this Series

1

"Crap," I hissed to myself as I almost tripped over an empty cardboard box.

My feet caught up to me as the female witch checked over her shoulder to make sure no one was following her. Erm, sorry witch.

"No, I don't know anyone who's interested," she said into her phone.

She stood in front of the small independent cinema, waiting for the doors to open. It was the middle of the week at the time between work and going out. Most people would be polishing their appearances, but not me. No, I was tailgating a young

1

witch who had the intelligence of a mouse. Wait, that wasn't very fair on the mouse.

"I told you to leave me alone."

Standing against the wall on the opposite side of the road, I was tucked behind railings that led to the front door of a town house. Just out of sight.

The witch was a person of interest in the most recent case of the Hunted Witch Agency. Okay, so maybe I shouldn't have been out hunting on my own, but I was bored. When Justina had ordered me to take a week off to recover from my loss of witch magic, I might have rebelled a bit.

"I'm not doing it again. The way you treat people, its vile!"

Oh, witchy knew a posh word. Maybe it was time I approached her to find out exactly who she was talking to. Her file had warned me that she was connected to the London coven, so she had a lot of protection. However, her previous befriending of a couple of the witches that had gone missing made her a person of interest. And hearing her conversation, I would bet my life that the person on the other end of the phone was a leader in the slave trade ring.

The doors to the cinema opened, a young male employee grinning at the witch as she slipped inside. Her blonde ponytail swung as she laughed at something he said. She had obviously been there before, plenty of times.

Sliding out from my hiding place, I crossed the road, my hand automatically tapping my black leather jacket to make sure my dagger was still there. It had become a habit, especially since my witch magic had been severed.

Shaking my head, I ignored the pang that settled in my chest. Denial was a beautiful thing when whatever it was you were denying didn't catch up to you.

"There's my favourite partner," a deep voice said from behind me.

My footsteps faltered just as they landed on the pavement in front of the cinema. The skin on my arms prickled, making me want to rub them. But, I wouldn't. I couldn't show weakness to Gerard. Ever.

"What are you doing here?" I said without turning.

If I saw his face, my demeanour would crumble, and I wouldn't be able to hold myself together. Because, you know, I'd been doing a great job all week.

"I'm checking up on you. I thought I might have heard from you at least once." His sulky tone made me slowly turn.

"Well…" I sucked in a breath as I faced him. "…I'm not surprised you missed me. It's quite common for anyone who gets to know me."

He stood with his hands in his jeans pockets. His black shirt hugged his muscles, right where my arms should be. And, yet, I couldn't bring myself to go near him. Not that I'd have any right to touch him, we'd only shared one kiss.

"How are you?"

There it was… the pity. Ugh. That was exactly why I hadn't wanted to speak to anyone from the agency.

Biting my bottom lip, I ran my gaze over his hair. Mousey brown, sticking up on top, short at the sides. His lips, a little full, but not too much. The line of his jaw, strong, clenched almost all of the time. And those grass green eyes. Big, but not enough to remind me of an alien. He was just plain hot.

"I'm… going to watch a film, so I'll have to catch up with you later."

Ignoring the wave of his tattooed arm as he tried to stop me from leaving, I stormed through the doors.

The foyer wasn't very busy, the rush of people not expected for another thirty minutes. A pretty tune played in the background, reminiscent of traditional movie theatres. It wasn't often a little gem like this place still existed. It was a treat.

"I'll join you, then." Gerard.

His scent wafted up my nose as he came to stand next to me. I ignored him as I checked to see if the other witch was still around. I couldn't see her. Great, not only was my partner bugging me, he had made me lose my target.

"Devon." Gerard grabbed my arm as I was about to go looking for the witch. "What's going on with you?"

A steward watched us from a few feet away, his hand on his walkie talkie. Okay, I didn't need any drama inside the cinema. I wanted to find my witch, interrogate her, and get on with my day. Why was Clingy Macsmellgood being so... clingy?

"I'm following a lead," I bit through my teeth. "Will you just act cool?"

He let go of me as he checked around us. Offering the steward a smile, I went over to the ticket booth and ordered two to see some paranormal film. Typical. Humans always made vampires and werewolves out to be romantic. If only they had seen the real thing.

5

"You're not supposed to be working," Gerard said, following me to the snack counter.

Well, if in Vegas, or whatever the saying was. Ignoring him, yet again, I ordered a small stack of treats.

"Are you trying to get diabetes?" His wide eyes were comical as I walked away from him, a small smile tugging at my lips.

I was having a mid-twenties crisis, he knew that. In fact, since my witch magic had severed when I attacked the crazy old lady, I'd been feeling even worse than before.

"I'm trying to drown my sorrows. You're not helping."

Moving towards the corridor where the screens were, I heaped my ton of treats into Gerard's arms. Without saying a word to him, I disappeared into the ladies. First, to check if the witch was in there. Second, to get away from the nagging.

Going into a stall, I sat on the lid of the toilet, burying my head in my hands. Seeing Gerard had brought me straight out of denial. He had cradled me to him when it felt like I was dying. He had taken me home and tucked me up, refusing to leave me until I promised that I was okay. Which I wasn't.

I was a warlock. I was the leader of a coven of creatures who hated me. I was... lost.

"No, I won't work with them again." The voice echoed around the bathroom as the girl I had been stalking came in.

Freezing, I lifted my legs off the floor and tucked them on the seat. Listening for clues would be my best bet. Then, I would ask her my own questions.

My breath was slow, silent, as I stayed completely still, balanced precariously on the lid of the toilet. It was a good job I was so small. Sometimes, just sometimes, being five foot came in handy.

"They threatened to kill my family. I have to be careful."

The tap came on, drowning out her words. Crawling off the toilet, I quickly unlocked the stall and peeked out. Ponytail girl was staring at her reflection in the mirror. Her cheeks were red, her eyes glassy.

Switching off the tap, she ran a hand over her face. "You need to help me get a fix. I'm here now, let's meet."

Oh, so the girl had a drug problem of some sort. That wasn't surprising. Some underground creatures helped others to get drugs, even sometimes getting them addicted to a hit of magic, or blood, if vampires were involved.

When she looked up into the mirror again, her gaze traced behind her. I kept completely still, hoping she wouldn't catch my eye watching her through the tiny crack of the door and its frame.

"I swear," she carried on, drying her hands on a paper towel. "I feel like someone's watching me all the time."

Swinging her ponytail, she left the bathroom, still on the phone. Coming out, I went after her, ready to apprehend her. She knew something about the slave trade, I just felt it in my gut.

Thumping straight into Gerard on the other side of the door, I swore under my breath. He dropped my sugary treats all over the floor as I barged into him.

"Pick them up!" I demanded before following blonde ponytail girl down the corridor.

"Wait!"

Ignoring him, I tucked my hair behind my ear, keeping a safe distance from my prey. She had put her phone away, glancing over her shoulder just as I pretended to stop and read a poster on the wall. If I looked suspicious, she would bolt. I didn't want her to do that.

"Devon! Stop pissing around and talk to me." Gerard's sharp tone tipped the scales.

The girl looked over her shoulder, saw him striding down the corridor and pegged it out of there. Her legs carried her to the fire exit. Going after her, I thought about throwing a barrier spell around the building to stop her from escaping.

My feet slowed as I realised that I could no longer do that. Witch magic was no longer a part of my talent stream. I was useless. I didn't want to use my warlock magic to stop her, it would hurt. A lot.

Killing the girl wasn't part of my plan, so I had to let her go. Watching her back retreat from the building, I kept walking, my boots dragging as my fingers traced the wall for no reason.

Gerard's footsteps thundered behind before he came to stand right in front of me. "Who was that?"

"I told you," I said, looking at the floor. "A lead."

His hand came to my chin, trying to nudge it up. Ripping away from him, I growled as I stepped away. "Leave me alone! You just made me lose her!"

Why was I angry at him? What had he done? For the week since I had become a full warlock, he had tried to contact me, even coming to the apartment. I had avoided him at all costs, hiding away and pretending that I wasn't there.

I shouldn't be mad at him, but for some reason, I was. Even the thought of Justina wound me up. It felt like she had deemed me unfit for work, sending me packing. When I needed them the most.

"Justina asked me to come and fetch you back to work. I'm not sure if you're ready."

His grim expression made me grit my teeth. How dare he assume that he knew when I was ready to work? He didn't know me. He...

A lump came to my throat as my denial burst open. I was a warlock. No longer a witch. I had wanted to be a witch, had chosen to hand over the leadership, but my choice to use warlock magic had taken away my power. Forever.

"I'm ready to go back to work, just as you've seen. If you weren't here, I would've had a new witness." My huff of breath halted when he gripped my wrist with his fingers and tugged me closer to him.

Shoving his chest, I tried to get free, but he held firm. His eyes were clear, full of clarity. He knew something I didn't.

"Get off me!"

"No," he muttered. "You're blaming me for what happened. Blaming the agency for making you use your magic. But, you need to grow up. Stop burying your head and wake up."

"You shouldn't be a therapist, Gerard," I spat, wrenching my wrist out of his grip. "You're useless at comforting... me."

His lips pursed as he stared down at me. I stared up at him, daring him to continue his tirade. If he kept going, maybe I could throw a couple of magic balls at him. I'd just blame my childishness. He seemed to think I was a kid, so why not act like one?

Releasing my held breath, I turned away from him. I wasn't in the right place to deal with tough love. He could try all he wanted, but it wasn't going to work. I needed... I didn't know what I needed, that was the problem.

"Devon," his voice was tight, almost pleading. "I've been trying to tell you something. I think it will help."

Nope, that wasn't going to work. My whole being was numb as I slunk along the corridor, picking up the sweet treats from the floor. See? Gerard didn't know me that well if he hadn't even bothered to rescue what I valued most.

"Okay, fine, don't listen to me," he said, throwing his arms in the air. "I won't tell you that you're actually still part witch."

He came closer as I froze, my hands clutching a bag of chocolate. My eyes rose to meet his gaze as he approached.

"I won't tell you that I cast a spell to check your magic." His voice grew softer, his stare intent.

"And, I won't tell you that your witch magic is still hanging on by a thread. A thread so small, that it could break with just one use of your warlock magic. It's the only reason you're still alive."

2

"**I**'d forgotten that Becky, the seer, told us that I'd die if I didn't choose between being a witch and a warlock. I should've known something wasn't right when I survived."

Justina's eyebrows rose as I took a gulp of tea.

The kitchen at the agency was spotless, the metal and marble surfaces glistening from the sunlight that streamed through the windows. I sat at the centre counter, my energy high at Gerard's information.

I'd gone home the evening before, not believing my partner. But, after tossing and turning all night, I knew he had to be right. Which gave me hope.

Justina sat opposite me, her face softening when she saw how excited I was. She had welcomed me with a hug, which was unlike her. And, yet, as she watched me, I could see her thinking.

"What is it?"

Leaning forward, she rubbed her hands together before she spoke. "I'm sorry I sent you home after the showdown. I know you struggled not being here, but I believed that I was helping you."

My whole demeanour had changed from the day before. My sorrow, my depression, had lifted. I was done with feeling sorry for myself. If I had a chance to be a witch again, I wouldn't lose it. Believing that I was a warlock had helped me to see what I really wanted to be.

"It's fine," I muttered, a tiny bit embarrassed by my obvious sulking.

"You're fine now, but Gerard said that you'd been suffering. I hate the idea of that. You're a part of us now, even if you've only been here for a while. I want you to trust me."

Frowning, I flicked my hair over my shoulder. "I do trust you."

"Good."

"How are you feeling about Gerard killing Luis Camos?" I hadn't had the chance to see how my boss was doing since her ex had been slayed.

She had wanted to take him out, to get her revenge. And, Gerard had taken that away when he drowned the biggest lead we'd had.

Her head ducked forward, her hair covering her face. "I was angry at first. I might have been tempted to punch Gerard's lights out. Obviously I didn't.

"Shame," I sighed, sipping my tea. "He probably could do with his big head being deflated a bit."

"Now, now. He's been looking out for you."

No, my heart didn't flutter at her words. Not at all. I was just... Oh, who was I kidding? Having Gerard looking out for me made my skin tingle. He was a hot agent, after all. And... he had kissed me. Not that I'd even thought about our little tryst for weeks. Much.

Looking me in the eye, Justina cleared her throat. "After the witches were settled in hospital, I came home and sobbed like a baby."

The agency was Justina's life. She lived in the ancient old building that lined the River

Thames. It was worth millions of pounds. But, she would never sell it.

"It's good to let all that emotion out. Especially as Luis was connected to your dad in that way. That day was intense. I must admit, I..." Could I tell her that I'd also shed a tear over the poor souls we had rescued? Wouldn't it make me seem weak?

"Don't be ashamed. You're right, we need to express our emotions. If we don't, we hold it in and start reacting from it. Instead, we have to let it out. That helps us to get back into our professional headspace."

Almost laughing, I waved my hand when Justina tilted her head to the side, her lips pursed.

"I was just thinking that I've done nothing but be Mrs Mac-grumpy the last couple of weeks. Plenty of releasing emotions going on. Even if they were mainly sulking."

We both laughed as we took a biscuit off the plate that rested between us. We had somehow found a kinship, which had been rare for me.

"How are the witches?" I asked.

"They're recovering well. Some still have their magic, others lost it completely. None of them remember anything. They've been spelled to keep their mouth shut, just like Lilia was."

Kurt burst through the old wooden door, his hands full of flowers, chocolates and a small bag. He strode over to Justina, bent over and kissed her full on the mouth before standing up again.

I didn't know where to look as she blushed, her cheeks turning bright red. Did he have to show such a public display of affection?

"You're always moaning that I never remember your birthday. So, happy birthday!" Almost shoving the gifts into her arms, he laughed when she stuttered, unable to reply.

"Looks like you've made her speechless," I said, laughing when he winked at me. I had already given her a card and a mug that read *'I am diplomatic. After I've had my coffee.'*

"Good. Maybe it will keep her quiet for the rest of the day. Until tonight-"

"Kurt!" Justina's fist flew out and connected with his thigh.

Getting up from my seat, I nabbed another biscuit before backtracking across the kitchen. "I don't need to know about all that. Happy birthday, Justina. Erm... I'll just go and find Gerard."

About to turn and run, I froze when Justina called me back. Her presents were on the table. She glanced at them with a twinkle in her eye before looking at me.

"I've got a mission for you both. You're not going to like it."

Instead of feeling apprehensive, my stomach flickered with butterflies. I was ready to get out on a mission. My boredom, and maybe a little depression, had kept me in bed for the last week. It was time to get back out into the field.

"What's our mission?"

Kurt watched Justina as she fidgeted with her mug. He sighed as he looked at me, ready to deliver the blow the only way he knew how. "Go see your ex coven leader. Find out if she knows our prisoners. She might hate you but get the information we need."

Oh, great. I hadn't seen Theresa since she had chucked me out of her club. And, now they wanted me to play nice?

"Okay." My reply was short and sweet.

There was no point in getting uppity about it. Gerard would be with me, which meant he could do all the talking.

The others didn't stop me as I left the kitchen. My heart was pounding, my head

18

slowly starting to join it. I didn't really want to go and humiliate myself, but it had to be done.

Our prisoners were locked away in the supernatural jail, refusing to talk. I hadn't even known there was a place for underworld creatures to be held. It made sense, considering they had to diffuse all the magic in the place. The agency's structures were much stronger than human buildings, making sure vampires and shapeshifters were locked up tight, unable to use their super strength.

"Devon."

Gerard's deep gravelly voice echoed down the hallway from behind me as I headed towards the library. Pausing, I turned to face him as he approached. A small smile came to his mouth when I grinned, happy to be back.

"I see that my news had a positive effect. Are you ready to go and question Theresa?"

Frowning, I ran my fingers through the end of my hair. "I suppose so. Although, I'm not happy about it. It's going to be really awkward. So, you can be Mr Agent Nice-guy."

"Not Mac-dreamy pants?"

My mouth dropped open in mock horror. "I never thought of that one. It's good."

19

Moving to leave at the same time, I laughed when we bashed into each other. Gerard caught hold of my waist, the touch making me suck in a breath.

"I'm glad you're not mad at me anymore." His fingers brushed against my skin as he slowly pulled away.

Swallowing, I bit my lip as I followed him out of the front door. "I am still mad at you. Very mad. Do you know how upset I was that you dropped all my sweet treats?"

My words were ignored as he marched along the bank of the Thames. I had forgotten how much I enjoyed seeing the back of Gerard. Not because I didn't want to see his pretty face, but because his butt always looked good-

"Stop checking me out and get a move on. We've got a busy day."

Ah, Serious Mac-agent had come out to play. I kind of liked it when he took control. It made me feel like I was protected.

"You do all the talking. If I say anything, I'm going to annoy her."

He slowed his step, his powerful stride almost faltering. "You? Annoy someone? Surely, that's not possible?"

I was about to answer when he reached out and took my hand, flashing us directly outside Theresa's club. It was the morning; the place was locked up tight.

Gerard glanced down at me, his bright green eyes sparkling when the sun hit them. I stared, unable to look away as his square jaw clenched. The tips of his hair were gelled upwards, the sides and back shorter than the last time I'd seen him. Why did he have to be so handsome? In a witchy kind of way?

"You're an agent. You have to learn to put all personal feelings away when we're in the field. We'll both question her."

His serious expression made me want to laugh, but I didn't. I held on long enough for him to move towards the front door. Smiling to myself, I straightened my back and went with him, ready to interrogate the bitch who had rejected me. Okay, that wasn't exactly how a professional thought. But, she was a bitch. There was no denying that.

"Why are we here?" I asked.

I had been so busy studying Sexy Mac-partner man, I hadn't thought about why he had flashed us to the club. "Theresa will be..."

Looking at my phone, I clocked the time. Ah, the coven always had a meeting, every morning. I had never gone, obviously. And, that was probably another reason I had been thrown out.

"Well?" Gerard said as I scrolled through my phone.

"Sorry," I muttered, concentrating. "I'm trying to find the address."

Almost cheering when I found the bulletin that Theresa had posted on the coven's secret website, I spun away from Gerard, ready to march down the road.

His footsteps followed me as the crowds thickened. The tourists were on their way to see our famous city. And, yet, none of them realised that hordes of supernatural beings roamed among them, ready to take advantage.

"It might be quicker if we flash there," Gerard said.

My fingers tingled at the idea of being able to use witch magic again. The whole of my body vibrated with the need to utilise the energy within me. Holding on to all the magic I had was making me on edge. I hadn't even realised until Gerard just reminded me that I couldn't teleport anymore.

"Hyde Park. They're holding their morning meeting there."

Holding out my hand, I looked down at Gerard's extended arm, his tattoo's moving with him. The reminder of why he had them came crashing into my mind.

"The seer said that you need to face... this." Waving my hand towards the numbers that lined his arms in different font artwork, I tried not to back down when he recoiled, his arm retracting from me.

"Another time, Devon."

His curt remark was followed by him grabbing my arm and moving us to Hyde Park. The dewy grass bounced under my feet when we landed. There were several dog walkers and joggers, not even looking at us as we appeared.

"There," he said, completely ignoring our weird moment. "That looks like a coven of witches."

Switching my agent mode on, I looked to where he was pointing. Yes, Theresa stood in front of several witches as they sat on the ground, their butts resting just slightly above the grass. They were using magic in broad daylight. Okay, that was hypocritical considering we had just appeared out of nowhere, but we weren't hovering just above the ground in order to stop ourselves from getting wet.

"Wait..." My mind raced as I turned to Gerard. "What coven do you belong to?"

I couldn't believe that I'd never asked him before. I'd known him for a month or so and didn't know hardly anything about him. Part of that was because I'd never asked.

"I don't. I'm a lone agent. I thought I'd told you that?"

Looking away, I tried to play it cool. Maybe he had, maybe he hadn't. How had I forgotten either way? "I'm sorry, I've been so wrapped up in myself."

My face screwed up as I looked at my pretty leather buckle boots. It was true. It seemed to be a habit of mine, only thinking about myself. I'd had to fend for myself for so long, it had become natural.

"It's fine. Let's just get back to our mission, shall we?"

Nodding, I shook myself and joined him as we marched towards the coven. There were around twenty people sitting in front of Theresa. On the edge of their little group, Jeremy, the witch I had almost killed, stood on guard. Spotting us, he visibly shuddered. Good, he was afraid of me. It was better that he believed that I could attack him again. Even though I was strictly on a magic ban. Which sucked.

As we drew nearer, the whole coven turned to watch us approach. Their expressions were reserved, hard to read. If they kept calm, there would be no problem. If they tried anything, Gerard would have to hold them off.

"What can we do for you?" Theresa called, her voice travelling to us.

The inside of my body quivered with anxiety. Why did my old friends put me on edge? I was an agent now, standing beside a kickass man who knew what he was doing. And, there I was, frightened that they would say something to make me feel small. To take me back to when I was a kid.

"We're here to talk to you. Alone." Gerard wasted no time stepping around the group.

Jeremy trotted after him, scowling in my direction when I went to follow. A barrier blocked me from moving forward when I tried. They had allowed Gerard to go to the leader, but I was kept away. Typical.

"I'm an agent from the Hunted Witch Agency," I almost shouted, trying to keep my temper under control. "I'm here on business only."

The heads staring at me turned to Theresa. Waving her hand, she dropped the barrier spell, allowing me to join my partner as he stood by her side.

"Can we talk in private?" he asked.

The middle-aged woman traced him with her gaze, her cheeks turning slightly pink. Was she crushing on my... friend? Yes, friend. Work partner. That's all he was.

Turning to her group, she dismissed them. Some of them left, while most of them huddled around, waiting to see what would happen. I didn't blame them, they'd probably been curious about what had happened to me. Especially considering I had always been the gossip among the covens my whole life.

"What can I do for you?" Theresa asked Gerard, completely ignoring me in the process.

I glanced at Jeremy who stood beside her, his stare full of hatred. He was lucky to be alive. If I could've gone back, I would've done the job properly. His rotund stomach was forced into jeans, the top overflowing. He rested his fingers there, tapping them in a rhythm.

Trying my hardest not to shudder when he licked his lips, I focused on my old leader as she denied any knowledge of the slave ring.

"Do you know these people?" Gerard held up three photographs of our prisoners.

One man and two females. Justina had interrogated them many times, but they were willing to die instead of giving away any information. It was a good job she did the questioning. I would probably have killed the woman who had been the cause of my anguish. She had been a powerful witch. One that had almost killed me.

"No, I've never seen them before." Theresa didn't even look at their faces, what a surprise.

Holding back from demanding that she looked closer, I trusted Gerard to handle it. He was a lot more experienced than I was. I had to stop myself from allowing my emotions to take over. Although, if my fist just happened to smash into Jeremy's smarmy face, I would call it self-defence.

"Let me give you a piece of advice," Gerard said, taking a step closer to Theresa. "If you don't want me to arrest you in connection with the kidnapping of witches, look at the pictures and tell me the truth."

Oh, Gerard. The hard arse act suited him. My whole body heated as I watched him stare down my old leader. If he ever wanted to go bad cop on me, I wouldn't mind. I probably had a pair of handcuffs somewhere in all my junk.

Pursing her lips, Theresa held back her reply. The red tinge of her cheeks was the only sign that Gerard had pissed her off. Her gaze slowly moved to the raised photos, her eyes blank as she studied the faces.

"Nope, don't know them."

Ah, crap, she was telling the truth. Gerard could also read her, his arm dropping. "And, what about you?"

He tilted his head as he looked at Jeremy. The creep was still staring at me, trying to intimidate me. If he even dared to-

"She's lucky she's still alive," Jeremy muttered when he noticed that my partner was staring at him. "She almost killed me."

"What she does outside of work is no concern to me." Gerard didn't look away when Jeremy's back straightened. "I'm more worried about how you're eyeing her as if she's a piece of meat."

My eyes almost popped out of their sockets as Gerard reached out, his fingers wrapping around Jeremy's throat.

"Don't even think about it." Theresa's hand rose in the air. "I will stop you."

"Don't worry," Jeremy spluttered. "He won't kill me. It will ruin his career. And, I'll get to kidnap the lovely Devon and keep her as my slave."

A rush of heat ran over my veins as my heart rebounded off my ribcage. All the memories of the years of him threatening me

28

came to the surface. Raising my hand, I was about to suck warlock magic from the earth under my feet.

The crack of bone resounded before I could move, Jeremy's limp body falling to the ground. Gerard's eyes were wide, his nostrils flaring as he breathed, trying to control his temper. Not that it had helped.

Theresa dropped to the ground to shake Jeremy's prone body, a cry escaping her mouth. No. What had just happened? Our mission had completely and utterly failed, even if a tiny part of me was glad that Jeremy had got what he deserved.

"Let's go." Snatching Gerard's hand, I pushed him, trying to jolt him out of his rage.

A huge breath sucked into him as he squeezed my fingers. Looking down at Theresa, his gaze cleared as he blinked. "I'm sorry."

As she turned to look at him, he flashed us away. It was a good job; her gaze had been murderous. Rightly so.

Landing in the hallway of the agency, we both stumbled, our bodies in shock. Why had Gerard killed Jeremy?

"I'm sorry," he whispered. "I'm so sorry."

His body shook, his gaze darting as he checked around us. Sweat lined his forehead as he stared into thin air. I had never seen the strong confident agent so traumatised.

"What happened?" Justina demanded as she came out of the library. "I've just had a call from Theresa. She's threatened to kill us all."

3

"Why did you do it?" I asked quietly.

The front door closed behind him as Justina and Kurt left. They had ordered us to stay hidden in my apartment while they spoke to Theresa and calmed the situation.

Kingsley squeaked, wanting attention as Gerard paced the tiny bit of carpet between the sofa and the kitchen. Going over to my pet rat, I stroked his head, giving him a biscuit when he nudged me. He could feel the tension in the room.

"I don't know. He threatened you. I got the feeling that it wasn't the first time." Gerard's voice was rushed, panicky.

Where had Mr Cool gone? His demeanour was failing him, which meant I needed to kick him up the arse. Not literally, although, sometimes it had been tempting.

"Listen," I said, going over and grabbing his arm. "You need to calm down. I'm not sorry you killed the man. He's been trying to get to me since I was twelve. I-"

Growling, Gerard shoved away from me and threw his fist straight into the wall. The plaster cracked, sending white powder flying around us.

"It's okay," I shouted.

He was breathing fast, hard. Taking his arm, I tugged him with the aim to get him to stop pacing. Instead, we lost our footing and fell to the floor. My head bumped on the carpet as his heavy weight landed on me.

"What are you doing?" he muttered, his face against my shoulder. "If you wanted to get me into bed, you only had to ask."

A chuckle rose before I could stop it. It wasn't a laughing matter, but my attempt at calming him had broken his aggressive spell. I hadn't ever seen Gerard so riled up. Had something happened to him?

Coughing from the dust that settled on us, I put my hands under me, on his chest and pushed. "I was trying to get you to see sense."

"Oh, right..." Lifting his head, he stared into my eyes, going silent.

We breathed, our chests moving in unison. Oh boy, it was not the right time to be getting intimate with my agent partner. He was having a murderous breakdown, and I was still trying to work out how to get my witch magic stronger.

"You were going to hurt him with your warlock power. I told you, if you do that, you'll die."

Shoving him, I scurried to my feet when he sat back against the sofa. Glancing at his arm, he pointed at a patch of bare skin.

"Wait, you killed him because you were afraid I was going to die?"

Surely not. And, if he even dared say anything about getting a tattoo for Jeremy, I would... probably do nothing.

Running his hands over his head, he sighed. "Yes. It was impulsive. A mixture of preventing you from using your magic. And, rage that he looked at you like that."

Confused, I went over to Kingsley's cage and took him out. Letting him nuzzle into my neck, I lowered myself onto the sofa next to where Gerard leant against it.

"No need to be so jealous. It's not like we're dating or anything."

Hothead Mac-sexy didn't find my joke amusing. He rolled his eyes, looking away when I tried to see if what I'd said had caused a reaction. Of course it wouldn't. I wasn't a full witch, we weren't allowed to date. Not only that, we were both messed up. Big time. Well, him more than me, just to be clear.

"So... We just have to sit here and wait until we're allowed out?" My skin warmed as Kingsley fell asleep against my neck. He could always comfort me.

"Justina is probably going to fire me. I'm surprised she hasn't done it already." Gerard's sigh was pathetic as his head dropped back against the sofa.

Closing my eyes, I allowed the warmth of Kingsley's energy soothe my erratic heartbeat. If Justina had any sense, she would sack Gerard. However, I had a feeling she wouldn't. He was her best trained agent, someone who had brought in the evillest of witches.

"You need to get a grip. Just because Jeremy looked at me like that, doesn't..." My sentence trailed off as Gerard's hands gripped his thighs tight. "Okay, you need to explain."

Turning to face him, I forced him to look at me. He heaved a sigh before staring up at the framed spell on my ceiling. Justina had asked me to take it into the agency to be studied against the one she had found with Luis Camos. The deceased man had somehow managed to get hold of a page from my mother's grimoire.

"My sister..." He took a deep breath, keeping his gaze averted from mine. "...was attacked."

He had a sister? How did I not know that? My insides started to shake as I realised that Gerard hadn't just killed his friend by accident. He had obviously seen a lot of trauma in his life.

"I was forced to watch, held down by a bunch of warlocks. They took advantage of her, right in front of my face."

Tears came to his eyes, which made a lump come to my throat. I swallowed, trying hard to prevent my own tears from forming. He really had suffered. Staying silent, I waited for him to continue.

"The reason I killed my friend was because of my rage. I was using magic whenever I got angry, trying to control the uselessness I had felt while my sister was..."

Reaching forward, I slowly put my hand over his, gently pulling it away from where he pinched his thigh so hard, his knuckles were going white. He gripped my hand, finally looking at me. His eyes swam with unshed tears as he searched my gaze.

"Why don't you judge me?" His sudden change of subject made me frown.

Taking a deep audible breath, I stroked his thumb with mine. The small gesture sent a tingling sensation over my hand.

"Because... I know what it's like to experience trauma."

Thrusting away, he got to his feet. "It wasn't trauma, it was weakness."

Ah, okay Tough-guy Mac-frustrating, I'd play the game. Instead of reacting to his anger, I climbed up onto the sofa and relaxed in the corner. Kingsley was still resting on my neck, but he was awake, the energy too palpable in the room for him to sleep.

"What happened to your sister after?" My words were quiet.

Standing by the door of the kitchen, Gerard slowly turned to look at me. His breathing had calmed, his hands no longer fisted.

36

"She's fine. It took her a long time to come to terms with what happened, but she stuck a middle finger up to the bastards when she got a degree in science and travelled all over the world solving science problems."

The corner of my lip quirked, I couldn't help it. "Your sister...a witch...turned to science?"

Gerard's shoulders relaxed as the tension seeped out of him. "I suppose it's pretty ironic when you think about it."

Good, we had broken the anger cycle. I understood perfectly well why Gerard felt the way he did, although, Jeremy hadn't ever physically carried out his threats to me. So, why had he killed him so coldheartedly? It wasn't a question I dared ask.

Slouching onto the sofa, my partner put his head in his hands. The realisation of what had happened was taking a while to sink in to the pair of us.

"You probably want to be assigned another partner," Gerard started. "I... I've never acted that way on the job."

The idea of working with anyone other than Gerard made my stomach flip. For some reason, he was my grounding force. He understood my predicament. He knew me better than anyone had ever known me, and yet, we still hardly knew each other at all.

I was about to open my mouth to tell him my thoughts when Kingsley squeaked. That meant only one thing.

"Someone's outside," I whispered.

Taking my hand, Gerard muttered "*Invisique.*"

His magic settled over me, causing me to shudder. The caress of the energy was sweet, recognisable. And... I shouldn't have been basking in the sexiness of my partner's magic when there could be a threat outside.

Pulling me to a stand when the door burst open, Gerard guided us behind the sofa and onto the bed. A man walked in, his arms extended ahead. A gun was clasped in his hands, but the darkness that pulsed through him alerted me to his warlock status.

"Look for the dagger," he told a young male teen as he followed him inside. "She just pissed off the witches, so she won't be back for a while. Hopefully, she hasn't got the dagger with her."

I frowned at Gerard when he raised his eyebrows. Why would they want my dagger? It was just a weapon.

Kingsley was silent as he pushed himself as far into my neck as possible. I was glad he was with us instead of in his cage.

The teen grunted as he started searching through my things. I wanted to launch off the bed and strangle the intruders, but something made me hold back. There was something intriguing about what they were doing.

"Why do we even need to do this anyway?" The sulky teen had pockmarked cheeks and a gangly frame.

The man who accompanied him stopped riffling through my drawers and turned to him. "Why didn't you listen at the meeting? We were told that the dagger is a conduit for warlock magic. It can hold it without the earth sucking it away. You need to start listening."

The teen didn't care that he was being berated. Instead, he was holding up a pair of my granny pants. Oh no, seriously?

Gerard's body started to shake with repressed anger, but he managed to put a hand on my thigh went I clenched my fingers into fists. We both had to keep our cool. The information about the dagger was extremely important. How had Justina required such a thing? And, had she known its power when she had given it to me?

"If you're going to take part in our mission, you need to pay attention. Otherwise, I'll disown you. Maybe the witches will target you first." The older man scowled in the boy's direction, his searching paused as he took on a fatherly role.

My dagger was in my boot, which was on my foot, which was obviously on the bed with me. Thank goodness. My skin tingled at the effort it took not to attack the men rooting through my belongings. Gerard would have seen my underwear. And, that was not on. Actually, there were a few sexy pieces under the comfy pants, why didn't the boy hold those up?

"Yeah, yeah, Dad, keep on. You need me to be a breeding machine, so stop threatening."

Breeding machine? What the hell did the warlocks have planned? And, did Maxwell know anything about it?

Maxwell. Shit, I still hadn't passed over the leadership. I was technically full heir, but I didn't want the responsibility of looking after the likes of the two men uselessly searching my apartment. The quicker I did it, the quicker I could concentrate on regaining my witch magic.

"It's not here," the young man said, spinning to leave.

The older man came over to the bed. Reaching for my bedside drawer, he laughed when he opened it. My cheeks flared red, my eyes stretching as a giggle left his mouth. His son was about to come over when he thrust the drawer shut. I'd had to keep completely still the whole time, praying to Mother Earth that Gerard hadn't looked over me and into the drawer. A girl had to please herself sometimes, it was quite natural... and mortifying.

"Something's off," the man said, standing right beside us.

Holding my breath, I tried not to move a muscle. If either of us made a noise or made the bed rustle, he would know that we were there.

"She must have the dagger with her. This was a stupid mission, why would she leave it behind? Let's go to that meeting."

The teen stomped out of the room, creating the perfect distraction. His father stood for a second longer before following him out. They had left the place exactly as they'd found it, which made it even more creepy.

Letting my breath out as the door closed, I hauled myself from the bed, my whole body shaking. Putting Kingsley back in his cage, I went over to the door and locked it behind them. They hadn't managed to break the lock when they barged in, but access to my home was too easy.

"I need to move," I muttered, leaning my head against the door.

"Where's your dagger?"

Coming over, Gerard held out his hand. Seriously? Some vile warlocks had just touched my belongings, their hands all over my undies and he wanted the dagger? Ugh.

Swiping it out of my boot, I held it towards him, blade first. He raised his eyebrows, his serious face letting me know that he wouldn't bite.

"We need to follow them." Tucking my blade away, I ripped open the door and ran.

If anyone was going to violate me, I would make sure they paid. Plus, I was still their leader. Surely, I had a right to know what meeting was going down. And, after that, I would get my revenge on the pipsqueak and his father.

4

"*T*hat's Maxwell's shop."

My obvious statement made Gerard frown at me. "Do you think I was born yesterday?"

Tempted to thump his arm, I resisted. He might be handsome, but boy did he wind me up sometimes. Yes, I was stating the obvious. But, he had just lost his mind and killed a witch, so excuse me for thinking that he might need reminding.

The two men went into the shop, their gazes checking over their shoulder before the door closed behind them. Isaac, the former leader of the warlock coven, had been proud of his heritage. He had turned the negative traits of warlock magic as positive as possible. He had made warlocks swear to only use their magic for good. Fat lot of good that did him.

"Let's go."

Gerard grabbed my arm before I could waltz over the road. I frowned up at him as he stared down at me. His hair was ruffled where he'd been tugging on it ever since he'd killed Jeremy.

"Justina told us to stay at yours while she sorts out my mess."

Crap. Why did Gerard have to be so proper? I hadn't even thought about upsetting Justina. The lead was too strong. We had to find out what the warlocks were up to. It could affect the whole investigation.

"I don't want to upset her, but it's a strong lead."

Digging out his phone, Gerard offered it to me. "Okay, let's tell her where we are."

Swallowing, I gingerly took the phone after he'd dialled our boss. We would probably both get fired. Especially as we'd gone against orders, after Gerard had broken a cardinal rule.

"What is it?" Justina's curt tone made me cringe.

I was tempted to not tell her where we were, instead ready to pretend that I was inquiring about their progress with my ex coven witch leader.

"We were at my apartment-"

"Were...?" Justina's tone was cautionary. "That means you're no longer there."

Oh, boy, if this didn't incite disciplinary action, I didn't know what would.

"That's right. A pair of warlocks broke in. We hid ourselves, but they were talking about my dagger, and-"

"Your dagger?"

Great, Kurt was listening to me on speaker phone. That made it ten times worse. Justina was the good cop, which made Kurt the pain the in the arse, kick me up the arse, cop.

"Yes, I'll tell you all the information later, but they mentioned that they had a meeting to get to, so..."

I let the sentence hang. They were probably going to-

"Then, why are you talking to me?" Justina's tone was calm. Not what I had expected. "Get into the meeting, or spy, or whatever the hell you had planned to do when you obviously followed them."

"Okay, we'll meet you back at the agency when we're done."

They hung up without even a word of warning. They didn't want to see if we were okay, as long as we got on with our job.

"She was surprising cool about us going against her word. I'm confused."

Gerard snatched the phone out of my hand, ignoring me as he went over the road. I followed, my sexy boots dragging as I tried to deduce Justina's real feelings. She was going to fire me. She probably thought that there was no harm in me checking out the warlock meeting because she would kick me out as soon as I returned anyway.

"I don't know where you're going," I said when Gerard headed for the front door. "But, I'm going around back."

Not stopping to see if he'd heard me, I ducked down a little alley that led to my destination. My stomach surged, causing me to heave as I came to the little concrete area behind the shop. This had been where I had shot Isaac senior a few months ago.

"Smart move," Gerard said from behind me as I paused.

My feet refused to budge from the spot where Isaac had fallen to the ground, a bullet in his head. The bullet I had shot into his skull.

"Are you okay?" My partner finally noticed that I was on the edge of a breakdown, or at least a tear or two.

"This is where…" I couldn't shake the guilt that wrapped around me. "Isaac."

Closing his eyes briefly, Gerard waited a split second before he reached for me. Instead of giving me the comfort I was expecting, he placed his hands on my shoulders and shook me.

"Snap out of it. We're here to work."

His words had been quiet, in case anyone from inside could hear. And, just like that, I wanted to hit him. Which was good, it broke me out of my sadness. When all this was over, Psycho Mac-killer would get a beating. Well, if I still had the strength to give him what he deserved.

"Okay, let's go," I said, taking my dagger out of my boot.

The risk of losing my witch magic was too high for me to even think about using any of my powers. Physical attack it would be. If there was a threat, of course. Otherwise, diplomacy all the way. Justina was adamant, so I would listen to her advice. For once.

Tiptoeing up to the back door, I gently pushed down the handle, smiling when it opened silently. On the one hand, easy entrance could be a bad thing, but on the other, I was going to take advantage of their sloppiness.

Gerard followed, his gun in hand. His arms were bare, the warm weather making our leather far too hot and sticky. Something about the way he yielded his gun may have made it hotter in the hallway.

"Okay, please, can I have silence?" a voice called.

The hallway was small. A door in front of me led to the front of the shop, which was where the noise came from. An open entryway to my right led to a small kitchen. A toilet was on my left. There wasn't much room to go anywhere, so I decided to be brave. Or, stupid. Whatever.

Sneaking to the door to the shop, I peeked through the glass. Isaac used to have a curtain of beads over it to make it look pretty. In that moment, I wished it was still there. Looking through was risky.

Gerard nudged me in the back, letting me know that he was there. I wasn't going to move, I was too busy counting who was in the room.

They sat in a circle, ten of them. The boy and his father were side by side, watching someone behind the counter. It must have been the speaker. I couldn't quite see him. A bunch of others were all looking too, including the freaky pale twins who were Maxwell's powerful sidekicks.

My breath hitched in when whoever was in charge stepped forward. He was a tall dark-skinned man. In fact, he was the one that Maxwell had sent after me the first night I'd ever met Gerard. He was a bastard.

"I've brought you here today so we can confirm that we're going ahead with our plan." The man spoke, his voice loud enough for us to hear. "Maxwell has no idea what we're doing, and as I've warned before, if anyone dares to betray us, we'll take you out."

The others nodded, their eyes staring at him. A couple of the women were unfamiliar, their energy different to the others. I couldn't quite put my finger on the reason something felt off. To the outside world, it looked like the warlocks were having a meeting, but...

"Once the witches have mated with the warlocks, we'll keep them safe from their coven. That way, if they become pregnant, the other witches won't be able to tell."

My heart stopped beating. Well, that's what it felt like. Shock vibrated through my body as they nodded along, agreeing with the insane person. They were going to do what now?

Taking a step closer to the circle, the warlock, with his long leather jacket, opened his arms. "The witches are against us. They want to annihilate us, so we've found a way to make sure our existence can never be wiped out."

Did they seriously...? I mean, were they seriously...?

One of the twins put his hand up to talk. The main man pointed, allowing him the floor.

"Maxwell would never agree to what we're doing. He's a strong person, one that can always be trusted to look after the coven. However, if he insists on allowing Devon Jinx to take her time in handing him the leadership, we have to take matters into our own hands. All our ancestors are twins, so if we procreate with a witch, we should be able to have more twins. Which would effectively grow our little family a lot quicker."

Bile rose in my throat at the idea of having sex with one of the creepy pale twins. How could the witches do this? Surely, the warlocks and their threat of non-existence wasn't important to them. Although, a thought flashed through my mind as they started to agree.

I was part warlock. Would that mean that I would die if the witches were able to carry out their plan? Those inside the shop believed that having half-breeds would save the race, but how did they know that the spell wouldn't kill me off too?

Gerard's breath fanned my neck, making me shudder. My parents had been reckless, stupidly in love. Their choice to have a kid had severely affected both their lives and mine. Making a whole tribe of me... well, that would be a stupid idea.

"What if the witches go straight back and tell their coven?" the teen asked.

The leader of the little group scowled down at the young man. "It might be hard to believe, but we were witches once. Our magic changed, so we evolved into a different species, but Isaac forced us to become friends with them. There may be one big guy out there who wants us all dead, but most of them don't. Do you?"

The witches shook their heads, their postures confident, their conviction evident. A part of me understood exactly why the warlocks were making the choice to breed. The threat was very real. My ancestor's spells were powerful, ones that could easily wipe out a species. But... ewwwww.

Gerard nudged me when the leader told them that they would reconvene soon. Scrapes of chair legs against the floor warned us of our time to leave. They would be coming through the door any moment now.

My feet were quiet as I rushed out of the back entrance behind Gerard. My skin started to sweat when the inner door opened before I had closed the back door. A shout inside alerted me to someone seeing the door close behind me.

"Shit, run!" I told Gerard.

The cries of alarm in the shop made me sprint out into the alley, following behind Gerard. They couldn't see me. If they saw me, everything would be ruined.

"Gerard, flash us," I called.

He slowed, his hand reaching out as I caught up to him. I could hear shouting just as his fingers wrapped around my wrist and he blasted us out of there.

"Ouch!" I fell to the floor, my face planting against the concrete on the river bank.

The salt in the air made me sit up, my hand cradling my cheek where I had grazed it. Pain was throbbing in the bone, making me whine. Gerard knelt down next to me. Tugging my hand away, he checked the damage.

"Sorry, we were both in motion. I told you, you need better combat training."

Winking, he stood and gestured towards the agency building. I followed his gaze, not bothering to stand. Nope. The hard floor was comfort enough for me right now. I needed a moment to recover. From our violent landing, but also from the shock of what I'd heard.

"Gerard," I said, a realisation coming into my mind. "They... they're going to make more of me."

The corner of his lip lifted into his cheek. Shaking his head, he grabbed me under the armpits and launched me to my feet. "I know. You know what that means, don't you?"

I looked up at him as he bent his head towards me. My breath hitched in as he stared into my eyes. Oh, how I wished for some intimate moments with him. Just like this.

"It means we're doomed."

5

My hand shook as I placed the dagger on the kitchen side. If the warlock had been right, it meant that...

"I knew the dagger was a talisman, but I had no idea of its power. I just assumed it was a good dagger." Justina picked it up, examining the blade to see if there was anything unusual about it.

I had already looked, but I hadn't seen anything other than a dagger. It was silver with a handle and a blade. That was it.

"I don't believe they knew what they were talking about," I said, lowering myself onto a stool as Kurt came through the back door.

"You're both fired." His expression was half serious, the not very stern expression failing when he glanced at Justina.

She screwed up her lips, staring him down. "We do have to talk about the last twenty-four hours. It seems our best agent let his emotion trip him up. And, our new agent was... being herself."

Duh. I couldn't be anything but myself. However, I had gone against Justina's orders to stay hidden while they spoke to Theresa.

"I found out some pretty amazing intel on my escapade, you can't be too angry with me. I promise to be a good girl." I gave them both my best smile.

For some reason, I'd always had a talent for blagging my way out of things. It wasn't something I thought I'd have to use at the agency, but needs must and all that.

"You're a pain in the arse." Kurt was deadly serious now.

Ah, crap, my charm had backfired on him. Justina on the other hand was shaking her head, her blonde hair brushing against her strong chin.

"I can't have these indiscretions. Yes, Devon, we know that you're a bit of a loose cannon. I knew that when I hired you. Just because I've been lenient so far, doesn't mean I'll keep you on." Looking at Gerard when he placed a mug of tea in front of her, she grabbed his hand before it could retreat. "But, you... What happened?"

He couldn't look her in the eye. Killing Jeremy had been crazy. His emotional trigger had taken over. I had never seen him act so cool, calm and deadly. With just a flick of his wrist, he'd broken Jeremy's neck.

I was going to answer for him, but I changed my mind. I had just been told off, I didn't need to invoke anymore ill feeling. My partner was handsome enough to fight his own battles. Especially as he had much more history with the agency than I even knew about.

"I have no excuse. A moment of rage overtook me. He... he was ogling Devon like she was..." Shuddering, he took his hand away from Justina and retreated to lean against the sideboard.

Kurt stood beside the breakfast bar, where we sat, staring at his friend. "You killed a man because you were jealous?" For once, his bluntness took a back seat. "What an idiot." Or not.

"No, it's okay, Kurt," Justina said, putting a hand on her partner's leather sleeved arm.

"I know why that might have triggered something in you, Gerard, but it's not on."

My heart sank at the idea of Gerard suffering because of me. Yes, it had been his choice to kill someone, but-

"It wasn't just that. I was about to use my warlock magic on Jeremy. He's been threatening me since I was twelve. I'd had enough. Gerard saved me from myself."

Kurt ran a hand over his hair as he sighed loudly. "So, you were about to kill yourself by using your magic and severing your link to your witch side?"

Nodding, I bit my lip. Yes, my stupidity was soaring almost every day. Even though I was at risk of dying, I still put myself into dangerous situations.

"Right, then you're not allowed into the field until you sort your life out." Slamming the worktop surface with his hand, he looked at Justina for approval.

Air sucked into my lungs as she slowly closed her eyes, her disappointment evident in her expression. She needed us to be working the witch case. We were so close to finding the culprits. And, yet, neither of us had proven to be very professional recently.

"I have an idea that might help Devon," Gerard said, picking up the dagger.

We watched him as he spun it, making the blade land in his hand. Holding it out to me, he gestured with his head.

Taking the handle, I swallowed when he came closer. What was he going to do? I had no idea how the dagger worked. It kinda scared me.

"The warlock said that the dagger can contain your magic. Wait..." He quickly stopped my disagreement. "...hear me out. If you put some of your warlock magic into the dagger, it might be enough to help your witch magic come back slowly. That way, you're not left completely vulnerable."

Blinking, I looked down at the dagger. Okay, that could work. As long as my power wasn't too strong for the blade.

"What if it can't hold my power? I am pretty awesome, remember." My smirk was ignored as Justina got to her feet.

"No, he's right. If you put some of your magic in the dagger, it will stay there until it's claimed. You'll have to keep it on you at all times, or another warlock could steal it. But, it just might be enough to clear your connection to earth to access your pure witch magic."

"That way," Gerard continued, "when you give up being a warlock, you'll have enough witch power to work with."

Kurt grunted, his expression confused. "I don't see why you should give up your warlock magic. You'd be losing a part of your identity."

The silence almost echoed around the room as we stared at him. I had made the choice to become a full witch. My life depended on me choosing between the two. And several factors outweighed being a warlock. Dating Gerard wasn't that high on the list. At all. Probably. Just number two.

"If she doesn't chose, she'll die." Gerard's sharp reply made Kurt smile.

Oh, great, and now he was going to...

"You want her to become a full witch so you can bang her. I don't see a problem with banging her anyway. There's tons of multi-cultural relationships nowadays, just ask Devon's parents."

Emotional pain sliced my chest as a lump came to my throat. Justina stared open mouthed at her partner, her shock unable to even express itself.

Gerard shook his head before he looked at me. Taking my hand, he pulled me from my seat and dragged me out of the kitchen.

"Gerard," Justina called before the door shut behind us. "You're on probation from now on."

Clenching my eyes shut to try and clear the tears that had gathered there, I didn't take any notice of where Gerard was taking me. The cool air of the basement cavern made me shiver as my feet hit the last step.

"They're going to kill you," I muttered as I hugged myself.

He moved to the centre of the room, his boots kicking up a small amount of dust. "They'll do all the paperwork, but they need me working this case. It'll be fine."

Clearing my throat, I moved to join him where he stood, watching me.

"Do you feel confident enough to try and put some of your warlock magic in the dagger?" He asked.

So, we were just going to ignore everything that Kurt had just said about us, about my parents. Even though it was technically the truth.

"Would you...? If I...?" Oh, man, how did I ask him such a monumental question? "If I had lost my connection to my witch magic, would you still be attracted to me, or would you have-?"

"Don't," Gerard interrupted, flicking his wrist to light the torches.

The flames danced, even though there was no breeze. The power in the room was palpable. And, there I was, asking him about dating.

"Right now, all I'm interested in is helping you to be able to function as an agent so we can catch the ringleader of the slave trade. The rest of it, it's your choice. And, something that has to wait. If you stop being a warlock now, you'll be useless in our hunt."

Professional Mac-cold had come out to play. Fair enough. It had been a weird few days. It was time we got back on track. Our top priority was to save the witches who were being kidnapped and the warlocks who were being threatened.

"Okay," I said, going to the centre of the room. "Let's try this."

My whole body shook gently as I held the dagger by the handle, extending it in front of me. It was hard to imagine that it could work, but maybe if I siphoned some of my warlock power out of me, I would be able to build my witch magic.

I jumped when Gerard's hand rested on my shoulder. Turning my head to look at him, I frowned. His eyes were closed. A jolt of his magic jerked into me, making my eyes close. He was supporting my witch magic, just in case it didn't work. If I used my warlock magic, at least I could still hold on to that tiny thread that was still connected to the pure magic of the earth. Well, with Gerard's help, anyway.

"Thank you," I whispered.

Opening my eyes, I took a deep breath and tugged on the impure energy that ran under my feet. I envisioned a stream of magic that sucked through my body and came out of my hand. As soon as the yellow ethereal power hit my palm, it moved along the handle of the dagger and down the blade.

I gasped when it disappeared, leaving the dagger looking normal. Did it work?

"Try again," Gerard muttered.

Doing as he said, I repeated the process of bringing my magic through me and into the blade. Eventually, it started to glow a very slight yellow. My body was revitalised, energised. My veins hummed, like they used to when I had enough of both magic winding through me. I missed the feeling.

When I had finished, I reached up and laid my free hand over Gerard's. Squeezing gently before he pulled away, I smiled to myself.

Once our connection was gone, my body swayed. His hands came around my waist, steadying me. Tingles fanned out on my skin under my top where he touched me.

"Are you okay?" His deep voice was huskier than normal.

My eyes closed, my body tempted to lean back against him. Something about the intimacy of sharing magic made me want to surrender to him. And, yet, he stepped away as soon as I was firm on my feet.

"I think it worked. I feel weaker, but..."

Concentrating on the witch magic that was pulsing at my feet, I pulled gently, surprised when some of it poured into me. Tears popped into my eyes, squeezing out of the corner as the power flooded me.

"*Invisique*," I whispered, laughing out loud when Gerard gasped.

"It worked!" He laughed when I reappeared. "Be careful though. You still need to keep that balance."

The muscles in my legs wanted to move. I hadn't realised how weak my body had been. I'd tried to keep up with losing my magic, but until this moment, I hadn't realised quite how much I'd lost.

"What now?" I asked my partner, ready to get to work.

He grinned for the first time in days. "Now, we sort out the mess we've made. And, catch that son of bitch who has been eluding us."

6

"What the hell was that?" I shouted to Gerard when he paused on the other side of the road.

Something had been thrown out of a window of a car as it passed. Liquid had rained over several people, most of them dropping to the ground as they cried out.

"Shit," Gerard called. "It's acid."

A few splashes had caught my arm, but nothing serious. My skin started to burn as I rushed back to where Gerard was trying to help a man on the floor.

"Water!" he shouted. "Get some water!"

Spinning back, I almost got run over by a car as I sprinted across the road and pounded my fist on the glass of Maxwell's shop door. We had arranged to meet him to tell him all about the groups little plan. Justina and Kurt would be joining us in fifteen minutes.

The door swung open, the smiling huge-framed figure of Maxwell blocking my way. Trying to push past him, I almost gagged when my face somehow ended up colliding with his armpit.

"What's going on?" His booming voice carried all the way outside.

"Help her!" Gerard shouted.

Stepping out of the way, he gestured wildly for me to do what I needed to do. His tanned hand shot out and grabbed my wrist, just as I was about to go out to the kitchen.

"Your arm."

Not taking the time to inspect my own injuries, I yanked myself out of his grip. "We need water. Lots of water."

Without another word, I shoved my way to the back of the shop. In a way, it was handy, because I could see that no one else was with Maxwell. He was on his own, like we'd asked.

"Buckets are under the sink," he called.

Filling them both up, I grabbed mugs and floated them in the top. We needed to wash the acid off the human's faces as soon as possible.

Maxwell took one of the buckets off me as soon as I came into the shop. He followed, not even asking why we needed it. "I know who did this," he said when he spotted Gerard bending over a woman.

"Who?" I panted as I lugged the bucket to my partner.

Grabbing a mug, I filled it and went to a man who was sitting on the floor, cradling his eye. His cry of anguish was enough to make me yank his hand away and pour water over his head. The acid had almost burnt away his eyelid. Red welts covered his cheek, but his eye was ruined.

"Why would someone do this?" I cried, going to get more water.

Maxwell was helping someone else, dowsing their arm with a line of magic, instead of using water. That was interesting. And, stupid.

"I may have let the others know that you were coming here today. I promised them that a solution was ongoing and they expressed anger that I was allowing you into our territory."

Great, the acid attack had been for me. Just because I was technically their leader.

Or, was it that the group had seen me at the shop after their meeting? Maybe they were threatening me so I didn't tell Maxwell their plan. Either way, it wasn't going to work.

Gerard came over to check the guy I was trying to help. An ambulance had been called, but the man couldn't see anything out of his injured eye. It was too late.

"Move," someone shouted at me.

Kurt. He bent down to inspect my patient, taking out a small bag and laying it on the ground. Unzipping it, he picked out a pot of salve. "My friend, this is going to hurt like a bitch. But trust me, it will help."

The man's screams as Kurt smeared the clear gloop onto his eyeball made me heave. Looking away, I blinked when my gaze caught sight of Gerard's arm as he took some of Kurt's healing salve and spread it on a woman's chin and neck.

Going over to him, I grabbed his hand as he was about to use the last of it on her. He frowned up at me, his eyes blinking as I pointed to the huge red welt that spread across his forearm.

"Put some on yourself!"

My order almost went ignored. He was about to reach for the woman again, but I swiped my hand over his fingers and collected the pile of gloop. Holding his arm firm, I rubbed it over the blister that had formed. His sharp intake of breath made me smile. Good, it served him right for trying to play the hero.

"A couple of your tattoos are ruined."

He barked a laugh, his teeth gritting as I finished. All along, he'd been in pain, but he'd ignored his discomfort. What a bloody hero.

Pulling away, I was about to go back to my poorly man when his fingers intertwined with mine. Getting to his feet, he pulled my arm out, pointing at the small blisters scattered on my skin.

"You missed a spot." Taking some of the salve off his arm, he gently soothed it over my tiny injuries.

"Thank you," I said, smiling gently.

The noise of a siren made every one of us look up. We didn't have time to go to the hospital or to speak to the police. Maxwell already knew who it was, so we didn't need the police's help to determine the culprit.

"We better go," Maxwell announced, also anxious to get on with our meeting.

Justina tried to urge Kurt to come with us, but he wouldn't budge. "You go on without me. I'll go with them."

I bit my lip as I realised that Kurt Fielding, the bluntest person I knew, was actually a healer. The kindness he was showing his patients made my heart soften towards him. I had no idea who he was, not really. And, yet, something told me that he had a story to tell. One that I wanted to hear one day.

"Come on." Gerard tugged my arm, forcing me to cross the street with him.

The others joined us, leaving Kurt behind to deal with the ambulance and police. We would have to move our meeting to somewhere other than the shop. The police had a habit of doing door to door investigations.

"Hold tight," Justina said to Maxwell as she took his arm. "Let's go to Hyde Park."

Gerard flashed us both to a lake in one of London's most famous parks. It was habit for him to transport me at the same time. I didn't know if I was capable of transporting myself, but it was nice of him to think of me. Although, wasn't that a bit presumptuous? Not to allow me to try? Okay, it wasn't the right time to get on my high horse.

The birds sang in the trees behind me. I allowed their sweet song to filter through me as Justina and Maxwell landed in front of us. It was a weekday, with only dog walkers and a few tourists dotted around the park.

"Well," Maxwell said as he straightened his bright orange shirt. "I wasn't expecting all the drama. I would've worn better shoes."

Glancing at his Crocs, I stifled a giggle under my hand. The mud squelched under them. Trust Maxwell to wear the most inconvenient shoes ever.

Justina checked around us to make sure there was no one in hearing range. The park was where we'd encountered Theresa and her coven. It was well past their meeting time, but a twinge of guilt somehow found its way into my chest. My mother had been best friends with the woman. Surely, I shouldn't be so pleased that Gerard had killed her slimy sidekick?

"Are we here to perform the swap over of leadership?" Maxwell asked.

Oh crap. I hadn't mentioned to Maxwell that I was kind of scatter-brained. Although, he should already know that.

"I may have forgotten the spell," I muttered, trying not to laugh when his double chin wobbled.

"Then what is this all about?"

There would be a time when I wasn't in a war with Maxwell. I had declared that he could have the leadership, and promptly forgotten all about it in my drama filled life. Ugh. I needed to get a grip.

Justina stood back, waiting for me to talk. I was technically still leader, so I could see exactly why she wanted the burden to fall on me. Sneaky boss.

"Maxwell," I started, glancing at Gerard. He raised his eyebrows, but offered no support.

"Yes?"

Clearing my throat, I started again. "Maxwell, we overheard a meeting at your shop the other day."

The frown that furrowed his brow wasn't a good sign. It wasn't a curious frown; it was a furious one. "And, what were you doing at my shop? I don't remember you visiting."

This wasn't going well. For some reason, my puny brain had imagined that Maxwell would listen to me. What a very silly thing to think.

"Long story short, some of your warlocks tried to rob me. We followed them to your shop. They were having a meeting with others of your kind... and a couple of witches."

"Witches? In my shop?" I doubt that somehow." His chin moved more ferociously as his ire built.

Gerard tucked his hands in his pocket as he coughed. "Actually, I was with Devon. There were definitely witches in your shop."

Good. It was about time someone backed me up. Although, from the glare aimed at my partner, it hadn't helped Maxwell's temper.

"Anyway, the reason we're telling you is because they're planning something quite outrageous, to be honest."

Stepping up when Maxwell crossed his arms over his rotund belly, Justina raised her hand. "Get to the point, Devon."

"The warlocks want to impregnate the witches. They're going to build their own little flock of half-breeds, just like me."

If Maxwell had a spirit guide, it would be a puffa fish. His mouth opened and closed as his cheeks grew red. Why was he reacting so hostile? We were telling him the truth.

"Don't be so absurd! My kind would never do anything so stupid, except for your father of course."

Clenching my fists to my sides, I evened my breath. I had to stay calm, even if the bastard had just insulted my family. Maybe one punch to the gut would suffice?

"I'm sick of you finding excuses not to hand over the leadership. You're a disgusting little creature who should've been put down at birth."

I grabbed Gerard's arm as he went to move forward. He'd already killed one witch on my behalf, he wouldn't make the same mistake again.

"We're telling the truth," Justina said, pulling out her formal badge. "I'm here on business with Devon."

Waving her away, Maxwell focused on me. His dark eyes bulged out of his head. I understood why he might find me irritating. I often irritated myself. But, he had to believe that I wasn't lying. Why would I make up something so...weird?

"I've had enough of you." Lifting his hand, Maxwell send a stream of dark blue magic towards me.

Pushing Gerard out of the way when he tried to shield me, I held up both hands and muttered a barrier spell.

The magic bashed into the invisible wall, dispersing on contact. I almost cried out in triumph, pleased that my witch magic had held. It had been so long since it had worked so well.

"Stop!" I ordered Maxwell.

He ignored me, his breath puffing as he formed a ball and sent it flying towards Justina. She ducked, dodging it just in time.

Ripping out my dagger from my boot, I aimed it towards him. My eyes widened when flames of warlock magic that I hadn't ignited coated the blade. Ah, no, I couldn't throw that, it would kill him.

"Maxwell," I shouted, quickly glancing at Gerard and Justina. They both nodded, knowing exactly what I was thinking. "Until we meet again."

Flashing out of Hyde Park, all three of us landed behind the agency building. I almost fell over as my dagger clattered to the floor. Okay, the barrier spell had taken some of my power. I had to be careful.

Gerard went to pick up my weapon, only to drop it instantly. I couldn't hide my smile as Justina marched through the back door, leaving us alone. Scooping it up, I tucked my dagger away.

"What's the matter?" I asked my partner. "Can't handle me anymore?"

His face turned sombre as he looked down at his blistered arm. "It's not you I'm worried about right now. The underworld seems to be falling apart."

Leaving me to stand on my own, Gerard slunk inside. Sighing, I dropped my head back and looked up at the sky. Maxwell had overreacted. Or, had he?

Great. I had a feeling that Handsome Debbie Mac-downer might be right. The witch and warlock war was starting to spiral out of control.

7

Checking over my shoulder every five seconds, I counted my footsteps as I wandered towards our meeting place. When I had got home last night, I had snuggled Kingsley as I thought about what had happened.

Maxwell had to take over the leadership. Now. At least that way, if anything happened to the coven, it wouldn't fall on my shoulders. It might seem selfish, but if he wasn't going to believe me when I warned him about the danger they were in, well, there wasn't much I could do about it.

I looked over my shoulder again, just to make sure Gerard wasn't lurking somewhere. Not that he would be. He had no idea that I had arranged a private meeting.

"Woah!" a male voice said as I ploughed into someone.

Mumbling an apology, I looked up at the human's face. He was clean shaven, his eyes twinkling in the sunlight. He had a dog who nudged my leg with its nose. Bending down, I stroked its head, laughing when it licked my face.

"He's such a tart," the man said, offering his hand to help me to stand.

Taking it, I almost fell into him again as I jumped up. His pretty eyes were making me all giddy. That wasn't right. I was Miss Tough Girl. I shouldn't be getting all gooey eyed over a human.

"I'm Chris. What's your name?"

Ah, Chris. Such a human name. Such a human male. Every now and then, I wished I was normal. Being chatted up by someone who didn't have sharp teeth, or magic, or could shift into an animal... it was a relief.

About to open my mouth to reply, I stopped when my phone started to ring. My fairy tale human romance was abruptly ended when the theme tune of a classic, but quite modern, male strip film blared out. So embarrassing.

"I better go." My quick escape was regretful, especially as the lovely man and his dog watched after me.

"I'm almost there," I barked down the phone when I answered it.

Maxwell's chuckle was deep and extremely irritating. "Just wanted to check that you weren't getting cold feet, Little Missy."

His condescending tone made my blood boil. But, it was okay. I'd flaked out on him several times before. Not today.

"I can see your ugly arse now." My laugh was met with a growl.

His arse was currently standing outside a transport museum. Apparently, he was friends with the curator. He had often hired a room out for meetings.

"Well, hello there," he greeted me as I joined him.

Not bothering to acknowledge him, I went straight through the doors. There were a few people scattered around the place, checking out old cars and bits of trains. Very boring.

"I see you don't appreciate history." He walked beside me, leading me to a side door.

My palms started to tingle as I thought about the morning ahead of us. The other agents would be pissed at me for not including them, but their presence would only make matters worse.

Going through the door that Maxwell indicated, I paused when I got inside the room. My lips pressed together as I studied the layout. There were desks around the outside of the room, obviously Maxwell had dragged them away from the centre.

"I love history," I muttered. "Just not transport."

A symbol I didn't recognise was on the ground. Earth and salt had been mixed and spread out to create it. What was Maxwell doing?

Coming in behind me, he closed the door and locked it. My fingers itched to drag up some magic and threaten him.

"You look confused?"

His long fingers reached up to wipe a line of sweat away from his forehead. The orange jacket he wore was short sleeved, revealing his tanned skin.

"What is this?" My defence mode was trying desperately to take over. I had to stay calm.

Frowning, Maxwell moved to stand beside the symbol. Tilting his head to the side, he watched me. "You've never seen this?"

Slowly shaking my head, I waited for the obvious to become...well, obvious. No, I hadn't ever seen it, but something told me that I should know exactly what it was.

Sighing, Maxwell gestured to one of the plastic chairs. "I'll give you a little history lesson on our coven while you're here."

Er... really? I didn't exactly have time for learning. Plus, why did it matter when I wasn't going to be a warlock anyway?

Grabbing a chair, I turned it towards me and sat on it, leaning my arms on the back. I didn't want to get too comfortable. I hadn't planned on staying more than an hour. By that time, Gerard might think about looking for me. I was already a little late for work as it was.

"Isaac Senior was our leader from the age of eighteen. His grandfather was the founder of the coven, along with your great, great grandfather." Going over to a table, Maxwell rested against it. "They were best friends. They'd had enough of warlocks getting a bad rap because of their evil qualities. So, they decided to form a new coven and create a new warlock. They're the ones who live in London today."

My stomach churned. I had killed the descendent of my great, great grandfather's best friend. Ah, shit, no wonder my life was doomed. My ancestors probably hated me.

"Go on," I said, genuinely interested.

Clearing his throat, Maxwell put a hand on his round stomach. "They created this coat of arms for the coven. It's called Emendatus. It's the Latin word meaning reformed. They vowed to make amends for the evil that the warlocks had brought into the world."

Biting my lip, I frowned as I stared at the earth on the carpet. It would be a bitch to hoover up. However, one thing was bugging me.

"Wait. If they were so reformed, why do they still use the impure magic from the earth?"

Chewing the side of his cheek, Maxwell looked down at the ground. "When your ancestor and his friend tried to tap into the pure magic of the earth, they couldn't. The witches had claimed full ownership. Mother Earth had balanced herself by allowing witches to have pure, warlocks to have dark."

Woah, that wasn't something I had known. But, surely that meant that all warlocks would be forever evil?

"To answer the question that's running through your mind, yes... we do have evil in us. However, as you know, our code of law is so strict, we've trained ourselves to no longer give in to the temptation of the bad energy."

Maxwell stood, gesturing for me to go nearer. Getting to my feet, I almost froze when he waved his hand and a line of blue flames ran around the symbol. It was a simple circle with several lines running through it. Not like the pentagram, but not far off either.

"You need to stand in the circle and renounce your claim to the warlock title. I have a camera set up here." He went over to where his phone was on a stand. "That way, no one can dispute that the switch has happened."

"Why did Isaac choose you as the next heir?"

I had never thought to ask. It was obvious that I would be next in line, considering my ancestor created the new coven with Isaac's ancestor. But, where did Maxwell fit into it?

"My grandfather was the first warlock to ever sacrifice himself for his coven. He was so invested in the new way of being a warlock, he resisted his evil urges when it came to a life or death situation. As you know, not many of us do that. Even now."

Nodding, I stood next to Maxwell, not quite ready to step into the circle. "So, his ancestors became the third in line. Okay."

Laughing, Maxwell nudged me in the ribs. "No need to be so serious. You've never wanted to lead the coven. You're too much of a free spirit."

Sighing, I looked at him, seeing a man who was arrogant, smarmy, but also intelligent. I'd heard brilliant things about him before Isaac had been killed. I had to give him credit. He was probably grieving the man who had taught him...us...everything.

"I... I convinced myself that I wanted to become a full witch. The idea of losing my warlock magic, it frightens me."

His expression clouded, a confused look crossing his face. "Why would you need to become a full witch?"

Sucking air into my lungs, I faced him. It was time to be honest with him. Hopefully, just hopefully, my plan would work.

"You've known me as a kickass half-breed with magic coming out of all crevices."

"Well, I can't say I know you that intimately, but I'll take your word for it."

My bark of laughter broke the serious mood. Okay, so I had asked for that. I couldn't exactly berate him for my use of words.

Clearing my face, I held up my hand. A ball of flames appeared, bright red and pink. Maxwell didn't look impressed. In fact, he looked bored.

"Well, recently, my witch magic has depleted. Every time I use one type of magic, the other drains. If it's severed completely, I'll die."

His eyes widened suddenly, his hand gripping my fingers to dispel the magic ball on my palm. "Why are you telling me your biggest weakness?"

The sorrow on his face made me blink. Was... Did Maxwell feel pity for me? Oh boy, he better rein that emotion in pretty quickly, or I'd have to rectify the situation myself.

"You might not believe me about those warlocks going behind your back. However, what they're planning... It has consequences. My mother and father went against nature. They had no idea that their actions would lead to me having to choose."

Kicking the carpet with my leather boot, I swallowed down the lump that came to my throat. Maxwell patted my shoulder, his expression hardening when he suddenly gripped it. "You promise me you're not lying?"

Stepping out of his grasp, I held up my hands, closed my eyes, and whispered an illusion spell. The pure magic filtered from the ground and into me, but it didn't surge like it used to. In fact, as I pulled, the power started to wilt.

Dropping my arms, I wiped away the blood that had dripped from my nose.

Maxwell stared, his cheeks weirdly pale for someone so tanned.

"I'm not lying. Your people think they're saving their coven, but the babies created will suffer as a result."

I was the first half-breed. Warlocks were male. Yes, there were a lot of male witches now, but that's because they were created from parents who had pure magic. Some might dabble in twisting the magic into darkness, but warlocks had created their own magic a long time ago. Mother Earth had not allowed any female warlock offspring to have magic. They were human.

Maxwell bit his nail, wincing when he obviously hurt himself. His nails were right down to the skin. It was pretty gross.

"Okay, I'll investigate your claim. Maybe we could work together to find proof of what you're suggesting. The problem with covens, is the lack of trust in a leader. That's why you need to hand it over to me."

Glancing sideways at the symbol on the floor, I slowly nodded. "Okay, let's do this. I'm ready to pass over the leadership."

Lifting my foot over the flames, I stood in the middle. Digging my dagger out of my boot, I held it in the air. Luckily, no physical magic showed as Maxwell eyed it. I didn't want him to know that I had stored some of my warlock magic inside the blade.

"You start, and then, I'll follow."

Slicing the blade down my palm, I allowed a drop of my blood to fall onto the centre of the symbol. The earth hissed, a faint aroma lifting to my nose. Maxwell did the same, holding his arm out to me.

We clasped hands as our palms met. Opening my mouth, I took a deep breath before I stated my intention. "Mother Earth, ley line lore, I renounce my claim to the leadership of the Emendatus coven. I declare Maxwell Maddocks the new leader. So it shall be."

The flames around the earth symbol rose high, forcing Maxwell to drop my hand. Pain sliced through my head, making me grab my skull.

"What's happening?" I bit through my clenched teeth.

Maxwell groaned from outside the circle. I couldn't see him, the flames too high. If we weren't careful, they would set off a fire alarm. Just as my thought finished, they extinguished, and I fell to my knees, the pain leaving as quickly as it had come.

"Ouch." Maxwell was sitting on his butt, rubbing his chest.

My breath was huffing as I pulled myself up and brushed the dirt off my jeans. I felt lighter somehow.

"I think it worked," I said, stepping out of the circle.

Fumbling to get up, Maxwell swayed when he finally got to his feet. His big bulk almost stumbled forward. Helping him to get steady, I looked up into his eyes. Lightning bolts zipped across his irises, showing that he was holding back his magic.

"How are you feeling?"

A laugh escaped his mouth as he tapped my arm. "As if I've just taken a burden off your shoulders and placed them on mine."

The grin that lit my face was real. He really had done exactly what he'd described.

The switch had worked, which meant that Isaac and our ancestors had approved of the new leader. If they hadn't, it wouldn't have been a success.

"Maxwell, please, take me seriously when I try to tell you what's happening."

The sudden change of topic made him sober. He swallowed, his wobbly chin almost covering the movement of his Adam's apple. "I promise to listen to your advisement. What I do with my coven is no longer a concern of yours."

A sting of emotional pain flickered in my chest. And, yet, I knew that I couldn't be a part of the coven any longer. Not that I had ever played much of a role in it in the first place. Isaac may have trained me, but no one had ever really accepted me.

"Good luck," I said to him, patting his shoulder. "You're going to need it."

Moving away, I blinked as tears suddenly popped into my eyes. My back was to Maxwell as I made my way to the door.

"Wait," he called, forcing me to stop.

Turning, I smiled at him when he cocked his hip and crossed his arms over his chest. "You don't think I'm going to let you get away with it that easily, do you, Sweet Cheeks?

You need to help me with this so-called baby making grossness."

Waving my hand, I unlocked the door. "I'll be in touch," I said, smiling to myself as the door closed, shutting off Maxwell's laugh.

First, I had to get back to work. Gorgeous Mac-agent would be wondering where I was...

8

"Why would you go without me?" Gerard's questions were getting on my nerves.

Firstly, it was none of his business. Secondly, it had nothing to do with him. And, thirdly, it really was none of his business.

The night was warm, the summer evenings making it lighter than usual. People were lazing around, basking in the fun-filled London nightlife. Me, on the other hand, I was marching through the streets, yet again. With Inquisitor Mac-frustrating on my tail.

We were on our way to see Becky, the seer who had told me about my split personality, or you know, my witch warlock problem.

"Look," I said, spinning when Gerard tried to get me to stop. "Far too much attention has been on me. We need to get a lead on the witch investigation. After I've seen Becky, I'm off to interrogate the three stooges we captured."

He was about to speak when I put up a hand. "Yes, I have got permission from Justina."

Heaving a sigh, Gerard looked down at me, his hands on his hips. "I know you have, I was there, remember? She told me to come with you."

Ah, crap. I was so in my own head, I was losing touch with reality. Or, maybe I just hoped that Gerard would go away.

"There's the bar," he said, his hand taking hold of my fingers before I could leave him standing there. "Listen to me. I've got your back. No matter what happens, I'm here for you."

Doing an impression of a goldfish... Yes, my mouth gulped open and closed... I stared up at him. His green eyes were mesmerising as his tongue came out to flick over his lips. I had forgotten how sexy he was in all my drama.

Dropping my gaze, I brought my free hand up to trace the outline of the now healed blister on his arm. The tattoos under it were distorted. And yet...

"You got another one?"

The tender moment was ruined as I spotted tattoo number, literally, sixty-seven. Pulling away from him, I almost ran the last few hundred metres to the bar. Becky had wanted to meet out, considering it was a Friday night.

"Devon, stop!" Gerard caught, looking down as he walked beside me. "I can't help it, you know why I get them."

"Jeremy?" I spat. "He wasn't a criminal. He wasn't a murderer. He was a sad pathetic witch who only ever threatened. His tattoo will not clear your guilty conscience."

Ouch, where had that come from? Maybe my opinion on Gerard's weird tattoo fetish was harsher than I had realised.

"You're a fine one to judge."

I paused my footsteps, slowly turning to face him. He was right, I wasn't one to berate him for his weird killing method, but... I also wasn't hell bent on killing.

"I..." I couldn't say anything.

As I watched him, staring at the ground, it clicked. My view of him had changed. Seeing him snap Jeremy's neck so cold heartedly had made me wonder if I could trust him.

"I know that look," Gerard whispered. "My sister gave it to me when I couldn't save her. Ever since, she's looked at me that way."

My eyes closed, my breath rushing out. I was forgetting the reason behind everything he did. He punished himself for his best friend, he punished himself for his sister.

"Becky said that if you don't work through your shit, it will ruin you. I don't want that. I..." Forcing him to take my hand when he tried to refuse, I tugged him down so his face was level with mine. "...care about you."

His glare intensified before it softened. Our breath mingled as my hand held firm to the back of his head. He needed to know that I wasn't abandoning him. The same way he had just offered me his support.

"Let's stop letting our stuff get in the way of our job. Justina and Kurt are going to notice and probably fire us."

Blinking, Gerard pulled my hands off him, holding them in his. "You're right. I need to deal. I've been pushing it down, but since meeting you..."

"What can I say?" I said, nudging him with my shoulder. "I'm amazing enough to stir up all the crap."

He lifted one eyebrow. "You say that as if it's a good thing. I'm not sure it's something you should boast about."

Laughing, I dragged him towards the entrance to the bar. Becky probably wouldn't give me any herbs to make me high, so a beer was in order.

The noise hit me as we entered, the humans talking loudly amongst themselves. The smell of alcohol and sweat filtered up my nose. A typical Friday night in London City. In fact, it was nice to be around people for a change.

"Hello!" Becky called from the other side of the bar.

Worming our way through the crowd, we reached her side. She was all smiley, her cheeks bright red, almost matching the colour of her wine. Ah, she'd already had a few. So... How would she be able to help me?

"Oh, don't worry," she said when I eyed her glass. "I've already done the work. I just need to tell you what I saw."

Letting my held breath seep out of me, I lifted my shoulders and went to wave to the barman. Gerard extended a bottle of beer towards me before I could even turn fully. Wow, my respect for him soared as he greeted the seer.

"This may, or may not, be a celebration," Becky declared.

Frowning, I took a swig of my drink, pretty sure that it would not be a celebration. My pulse suddenly sped up. She had seen something. But, what?

"Don't keep us in suspense," Gerard said, checking around us.

Doing a little weird dance movement on her barstool, Becky held her arms out to me. Er, what did she...?

Leaning forward, she hugged me tight. Oh, that's what she had wanted? Well, it wasn't something I came across very often. Supernatural creatures weren't prone to being nice. Except Becky. The seer was feeling on top of the world, apparently.

"I saw the dagger," she whispered in my ear, her arms loosely flung over my shoulders. "You've stored your magic. I also saw a way for you to maybe, and this isn't a guaranteed maybe, find a way for you to keep both sides of your magic. To be both witch and warlock without risking your life."

Inhaling sharply, I almost ripped away from her. Instead, I kept still, allowing her words to sink in. Wait. If there was a way for me to stay... me, then I wouldn't have to choose. But, hadn't I already chosen? Wasn't that the reason I was there?

"I... don't know what to say."

Leaning back, Becky looked me in the eye. "If you keep filling your dagger with your warlock power for now, your witch power will grow stronger. Try and keep a balance. Let me work out the details. It might take me some time."

"You!" The shout made everyone turn and stare at a young woman.

Gerard stood in front of me when it became evident that she was pointing at me. Great. Who had I pissed off now? Was the girl annoyed at my awesome hair? Or, maybe it was the handsome agent that stood beside me.

The humans parted as the pretty brunette approached. There was a whole bar of people about to witness whatever this psycho bitch wanted to throw at me.

A sudden faint smell of gone off meat reached me. Gerard's hand came to my shoulder at the same time. He obviously smelt it too. A Dark Crawler.

"You killed me. Or, tried to."

Becky slid off her stool, ready to step beside me. Taking her hand, I pushed her back, hissing at her to leave. If the Crawler wanted revenge, it would probably jump into the seer. And, that couldn't happen.

"You're going to have to be more specific," I said to the Crawler as she got closer.

Stepping in front of me, Gerard shielded me as I bent and retrieved my dagger, holding it behind my back. That was the problem with warm evenings, there was nowhere to hide my weapons.

The girl was quite solid, her form not rotting badly from the inside. However, it wouldn't be long. A few weeks of looking good would give way to the bloated look of someone who had drowned.

"We met in an alleyway, you killed my body. Luckily, this beautiful girl was just behind you. You were so engrossed in yourself, you didn't think to check if there were any humans around."

Flicking her hair over her shoulder, the Crawler came closer. Some of the humans were still watching, but most of them had gone back to their conversations. They were sensible. It helped me immensely. Dark Crawlers didn't care about hiding. They were evil, detached. The police found it hard to capture them because of the hopping from one body to another trick.

"What do you want?" Gerard asked as I nudged him out of the way.

Pretending to rub my neck, I glanced behind me to check if Becky had gone. She had. Good, that meant she was at least safe from the vile thing inside the already dead girl.

"I want revenge. I know I said that I wasn't going to take over the half-breed, but I'm ready for a fight."

Oh no, it didn't. Did the Crawler just threaten to possess me? My fingers itched as I prepared myself. A smile came to my face as I took Gerard's hand. He looked down at me, frowning. Was it that shocking for me to want to hold his hand? Okay, he was right, I was going to use him for his magic. But... still...

Closing my eyes, I focused my attention on the girl slash Crawler. Whispering, I chanted the spell that I had used to trap a Crawler in my friend's grandpa. Yes, it wasn't my finest moment, but I wanted to make sure it couldn't jump into me. I liked having him around. Her grandpa, not the Crawler. And, I knew that as soon as it decided to leave, his sweet face would be gone. My mistake for caring about a human friend.

Gerard felt me pulling on his magic. At first he resisted, but after a second, he allowed it to channel through me. He had no idea what I was doing, but his trust in me made my skin warm.

"You can try," I said when the spell was done.

It was a barrier spell. It lined the human body the Dark Crawler possessed, not allowing it to jump out. Which meant that it would die as soon as she did.

The corner of the girl's lip lifted into her cheek. "An open invitation, I never expected that."

It was true that most underworld creatures detested the Crawlers. They rarely survived in the powerful bodies of any creature other than humans, but it didn't stop them from trying.

About to step forward, I was pushed to the ground by Gerard. He didn't realise what I had done. Taking two strides to the girl, he came to a stand right in front of her. "Take me."

My heart almost exploded. The man was protecting me like some warrior Viking. Now, that made a woman's heart flutter.

Scrambling up from the floor, I tried to move forward. An invisible barrier stopped me. Stupid Mac-hero was really taking his role as saviour a little too seriously. I couldn't exactly shout out what I'd done. The humans who were listening would think I was insane.

"I mean it," Gerard said, his frame tall in front of the girl. "Take me instead."

Cocking her head to the side, the Crawler laughed in a high pitched tone. Shuddering, I watched as Gerard opened his arms, offering himself.

"Stop it!" I tried to get him to look at me.

No, he wasn't paying attention. Luckily, neither was anyone else. I was about to try and push through the barrier when the girl brought a knife out of her bag. No. The Crawler might not be able to jump, but she could still kill my partner.

"Wait!" I shouted. "I'll do it!"

Bringing my dagger forward, I sliced it down in mid-air. Gerard doubled over as his spell was ripped in two, draining him of magic. The girl was still extending the knife towards him. Thrusting through the split in the barrier spell, I launched myself at Gerard, knocking him sideways.

He fell to the ground as the blade made contact... straight into my side. The Crawler was laughing as she gripped my shoulder with one hand. Gritting my teeth as hard as I could, I pushed the Crawler off me. The knife clattered to the ground as I held my side tightly. Wetness made me cringe as pain exploded. Son of a bitch.

Instead of staying for a fight, I kicked out my leg. My boot connected with the Crawler's chest, sending her flying back into the crowd. As she was swallowed by humans trying to help her, a man took hold of my arm.

"Are you Devon Jinx?"

I shoved away from him, staring at his familiar eyes. Who was he? Why did it feel like I'd seen him before?

"I can see that you are. Here, your father asked me to give you this."

Before I could reply, Gerard took hold of my ankle from where he was on the ground and flashed us to the agency. Landing on the lab floor, I groaned as darkness invaded the side of my eyes. Nope, I wasn't able to stay awake. Maybe that was a good thing.

9

"*T*hat bastard stabbed me!"

My exclamation was met with a grin from both Justina and Kurt. They were sitting in the armchairs of the living room. A television was showing a vampire show in the background. Really?

Trying to move, I cringed when my side twinged. The pain wasn't as bad as I'd imagined, but it still hurt like a bitch.

"How long have I been out?"

Looking around, I searched for Gerard. He wasn't there. Sighing, I sunk back on the sofa. I was laid out... again.

"About an hour. Kurt gave you some healing potions. You'll be back to normal in no time." Justina came over and sat on the edge of the sofa next to me. "You were clutching this when you got here."

An envelope was addressed to me, the writing familiar somehow. The eyes of the man who had shoved it into my hand before Gerard flashed us out the bar came into my mind.

Gingerly taking the letter, I resisted the urge to rip it open. I had no idea who would write to me, but I had a gut feeling that I wasn't going to like it.

"He... The man said that my father asked him to give it to me."

My memory came flooding back as I sat upright. Groaning when pain took hold, I grabbed my side, trying not to dislodge Kurt's patch up handy work.

Justina's eyebrows furrowed as I carefully opened the envelope. I ignored them, almost wishing that Gerard was there as I opened the folded piece of paper.

"It..." I stuttered. "...it says... Devon, for so long, I've waited to write to you. I told Isaac Senior to make sure that you were trained in your magic so you could be prepared for anything. However, I've heard that what you're going through isn't exactly what I was expecting. Please know that I never abandoned you. And, when the time is right, we'll see each other again. All my love, Dad."

My chin wobbled as I threw the paper on the floor. Who would pull such a cruel trick? Too many people knew about my story. Both witches and warlocks were aware of my parents dying.

Picking up the letter, Justina scanned it before handing it to Kurt. "Will you test it for authenticity, please?"

Nodding, he left us to do exactly what she'd asked. There was a non-written rule between them. One asked, the other did. It flowed well, unlike me and Gerard.

"Why would someone write that to me?" I looked at my boss. My friend.

Biting her lip, Justina looked at the ground. "I wouldn't right it off as a prank quite yet. Maybe your parents were kidnapped. It sounds like they were involved in something a young girl would never understand."

Clenching my fists, I gritted my teeth. "If they dared to abandon me..."

The door opened as I tenderly felt my side. It was nowhere near as painful as it had been only moments ago. Gerard sauntered in, a grim look on his face.

"There's a human hovering outside. She's approached the door several times but hasn't knocked. I have a feeling she knows who we are and has something to tell us."

Rubbing his now healed arm, Gerard slowly came over. His gaze traced me, but he didn't inquire as to whether I was okay.

"Well, since you didn't get a chance to interrogate the three witches, I'm going to head to the prison. Gerard, I trust you can take care of a human on your own?"

Reaching out for Justina's hand before she could rise, I squeezed her fingers. "I'm feeling a lot better. Please don't make me rest."

In fact, my wound was tingling, almost pleasantly as I got to my feet. Stretching, I lifted my top to inspect the wad of bandage over my stitches.

"Kurt's a talented healer, isn't he?" A proud smile lit Justina's face as she stood. "You can help Gerard, but no action. If anything goes down, don't defend him. He's capable of defending himself."

"I'm not so sure," I muttered. "He wouldn't listen to me tonight. I tried to tell him that I'd trapped the Crawler into the body, but he ignored me."

My partner's eyebrows rose as he crossed his arms. "Do I detect a hint of whinging?"

"Right, that's my cue to get on with it. Just… stay out of trouble, you're not technically on duty."

When the door had shut behind Justina, I took a step closer to Gerard. "You owe me your life. I was stabbed because of you."

Rolling his eyes, Gerard lifted his hands in the air. "You're infuriating. And… right. I should've listened to you."

A smirk came to my face before he could say anything to wipe it away. I would bask in my victory. He had never admitted that I was right. Of course I was right. It was quite a common occurrence.

"What did that letter say?"

And, there came the question that brought me back to reality. Straightening my clothes, I picked up my phone and dagger, and tucked them away. "Not a lot."

It was true. My father, if it was his writing, hadn't said much. There was hardly any point to his letter, unless he thought I would drop to my knees in gratitude because he was alive, when I had believed he was dead.

Gerard's arm came out as I went to go past him. His fingers brushed my wrist gently, forcing me to stop. He looked down at me sideways, his green gaze searching mine. The intensity of his stare made me look away. Confusion fizzed through me as his fingers moved down and caressed my palm.

"Thank you," he said, making me look up at him. "...for saving me from what I thought would be a Crawler takeover."

Yeah, yeah, I was a bloody hero. If only he would've listened, I wouldn't have been stabbed. Not that the pain was bothering me now, but it wasn't the point.

"Any moment now, Justina is going to call us in and discipline us for our not so professional behaviour. I'm not sure why she's holding off, considering we caused a scene at the bar last night. And, we're supposed to be talking to a human right now..."

Gerard's eyes widened. Letting go of me, he stormed out of the room, leaving me to stare after him. Since when had my life got so wrapped up in my job? We weren't actually working when we went to see Becky, but we had to protect the reputation of the agency. We weren't exactly doing a great job.

Following my partner, I swore to myself that I would once again put all my personal business to the side while I was at work. If I wanted to be a successful agent, I had to make sure I was professional on the job. No matter what happened.

The hallway was dim, the darkness outside making it seem even more eerie when Gerard opened the front door. I jogged to catch up with him, slipping out and shutting the door behind me. The pain in my side was almost gone. I would have to speak to Kurt about his remedies. Maybe he had a good one for hangovers.

The Thames was black, the lights from the bridges and buildings the only thing making the slight waves stand out. The street lights were on, yet, there was hardly anyone walking down the walkway.

It was the middle of the night in a place that was a little less touristy than other parts of the riverbank.

"She was just..." Gerard stopped talking when a human woman, about my age, came striding up to us.

Wringing her hands together, she stopped and stared up at Gerard. Her waist length dark blonde hair touched her butt as she bent her head back. She was short, although not quite as small as me. That would take some beating. A fact that I was pretty proud of.

"Are you an agent?"

Her lack of eye contact with me made me bristle. Did she think I was insignificant?

Which, obviously, I wasn't. Otherwise I wouldn't have come out of the same building as the man in front of her.

"I am. What can I do for you?" Gerard's warm smile made me narrow my eyes on him.

Was he flirting? I had never seen such a thing. In fact, I hoped he upped his game so I could laugh at him.

"I'm..." The girl looked around, finally acknowledging me with a nod. "I need to talk to someone in confidence."

Checking that no one was spying on us, I let Gerard take the lead. The girl was pretty in a sweet way. She certainly didn't look like she had all the flaws that I did. I could fill a room with mine. Not that I would admit that to anyone. Scratch that, I didn't really admit it to myself.

"Well, I'm sure we can accommodate you. Would you like to tell us your name?" Gerard tucked his hands in his jeans pockets, his demeanour calm and casual.

If he was hoping to give off the impression of not being awkward, he wasn't doing a very good job. I had never seen him act this way around a pretty girl before. Did he fancy her? Or, was he trying to use his charm to make her feel comfortable? Either way, it wasn't working. I could tell by the way the girl frowned. Time for plan B.

"My name is Devon," I said, offering my hand when it looked like she might back away. "This is Gerard."

The girl nodded, not bothering to take my hand. I didn't blame her; I knew I could be intimidating. Although, maybe it was just the fact that she was still more interested in Gerard. Whatever.

"I'd rather not give you my name. I know a bit about you. My friend… She knows about you, and she…" Chewing her lip, the human glanced towards the water.

A couple walked past, arm in arm. They giggled together, totally oblivious to the world around them. I'd never had that in my life. I'd had dalliances with a man or two. But, never had I walked along, my senses completely shot because of someone else. It was madness.

"Who is your friend? Does she need help?" Gerard looked down at her, a concerned expression on his face.

Ugh. Why didn't he just invite her inside for a coffee? Wait, what? Was that…? Did I feel a bit of jealousy? Oh, come on!

"My friend is a witch," the girl said very quietly. "If she knew I was here, she'd

111

probably kill me herself. She's friends with a very unsavoury person, but she's too afraid to come and talk to you. I..." The girl checked over her shoulder, yet again. "I'm afraid for her life."

Okay, this was serious. If a human was risking her life to come to us, something was wrong. Some witches befriended humans, myself included, but it rarely ended well for them. Case in point: my best friend was a human when I was a teen. I pulled her into my world when she asked too many questions. Ultimately, it led to her death. And, shit, it still hurt like hell when I allowed myself to think about it.

Rubbing my chest, I stepped forward, nudging Flirty Mac-smarmy out of the way. "I'm glad you've come to us. We work to make sure that all witches are safe from harm. Can you give us some information on your friend? We could find her and make sure she's safe."

Her eyes widened as she backed away. Gerard pushed me behind him, his deep voice husky when he told her to stay calm. "It's okay. I promise we won't let her know that you've talked to us."

Her eyes wide, the girl glanced from me to him. Her hand shook as she pulled a piece of paper from her bag. "I normally wouldn't go behind my best friend's back, but she mentioned something about kidnappings. She's not in a good way. This is my number and her address. At least I can say I tried to help her."

Shoving the paper into Gerard's hand, she spun away. Glancing at the note, I noticed that she'd written a number down. An address was also scribbled.

"Wait," Gerard called. "Who are you?"

Looking over her shoulder, the girl stopped walking. "You don't need to know. My friend's name is Lucia, and if you don't help her, she's going to die."

10

"I don't think I've ever been invited to this many people's houses... ever."

Flicking my hair over my shoulder, I smiled when Gerard eyed me sideways. We were in the cool agency van, driven by Kurt. Justina had insisted that we all visit the witch, just in case it was a trap. We would then make an excursion to the prison to see the three witches we had captured at the hotel.

Lilia, the witch who had helped us find the guilty witches, was tending to those we had rescued. She spent most days visiting them in their new safe house. We'd had to put them in protective custody to keep them away from the head kidnapper. It was a slave ring, alright, but someone would be the lead instigator.

"You're not technically invited." Loading his gun, he frowned when I reached out for it. "No, you don't get to touch this. This..." He gestured to the handgun. "...is a very dangerous weapon. Only those who are trained are allowed to lay a finger on it. You..." He pointed at me. "...are not a shooter."

Digging my dagger out of my pocket, I almost dropped it on the floor. A chuckle rumbled up his chest, making me want to take aim at his throat. Shooty Mac-hotty wasn't helping my mood. I had to stay focused.

"Have you drained some magic today?" he asked, suddenly turning serious.

Tilting my head to the side, I ignored him as I clung to the handle. Closing my eyes, I allowed my warlock magic to pour through me. A burning sensation filtered over my skin. Gritting my teeth, I let the power go as soon as enough had gone into the dagger.

Tucking the weapon away, I smiled to myself when the van lurched to a halt. I was about to comment on Kurt's reckless driving when he started to shout. Justina was in the front with him, but we couldn't see them from the back.

"Looks like we have trouble," Gerard said, jumping up from his seat and kicking open the back doors.

Pulling on the pure magic of the earth, I balanced my two sides out. The seer had said that she might be able to help me stay both a witch and a warlock. I hadn't even had five minutes to work out if that was what I wanted.

"Come on." Gerard's demand was urgent.

The shouting around the front of the vehicle was louder now. Justina's voice had joined in whatever conversation they were trying to have. Launching to a stand, my boots smacked on the concrete as I jumped off the van and ran around to the front.

"Stay back!" A woman stood in the middle of the road, holding out her hand.

We were outside her house. The address had been accurate if the threat was anything to go by. Her long dark hair was curled at the ends, her tanned skin perfectly smooth and clear. How typical. The Italian woman was gorgeous, if a little crazy.

"What's going on?" I whispered to Justina.

"I'll tell you what's going on," Lucia called, flicking her hand.

Pain exploded through my head as she cast a spell on me. The other three were also crippled by pain as Lucia squeezed our brains. Bitch.

"My friend had good intentions, but I know who you are. You killed my brother!"

Releasing the spell, Lucia stood with her hands on her hips, waiting for us to recover. I'd managed to get away with not being hurt when we'd caught the other witches, but now that I had more pure magic, other witches were able to harm me.

Glancing around, I clocked the suburban houses. The street was in London, but it was a council estate, tucked away in a nicer part of the city. People's curtains were twitching, but they wouldn't call the police. Humans and witches lived side by side, yet, the humans had no idea that magic was being used in their vicinity.

"I killed your brother," Gerard confessed, stepping in front of us. "It's me you should take it out on."

Lucia tucked her long well-groomed hair behind her ear. Now, she was a girl that Gerard was allowed to fancy. Her perfect figure was tall and confident. Her power was quite enhanced, which meant only one thing.

She was somehow involved in the kidnappings, like her brother.

"He wasn't a bad man," Lucia said, her lip wobbling. "He was all I had."

"He kidnapped witches and drained them of their magic. After that, he sold them on as slaves. If that's your definition of a good man..." Gerard shrugged, his facial expression blank.

Justina stepped forward when Lucia held her hand in the air. "Ignore him, he's a stupid witch. They get roped into things sometimes, don't they?"

Ah, the diplomacy police had arrived. I smiled briefly as I glanced at Kurt. He rolled his eyes as his hand hovered near his pocket. He was ready to draw his weapon, just like the rest of us. I sometimes wondered if he allowed Justina to have her way to placate her. Or, did he also believe that diplomacy was the best way to handle criminals?

"Exactly," Lucia spat, keeping her gaze steady on Justina as she moved in front of Gerard. "He didn't want to do those things, he didn't have a choice."

My whole body was tense as I waited to see what would happen. The street was empty, not even a car in sight. The energy in the air pulsed, too much magic in one place. Too many people on edge.

"I understand. Lucia, what those people did to your brother was wrong."

Justina somehow managed to tell the lie smoothly. Oh, I was liking my diplomatic boss this way. She loathed Luis Camos, yet, she was acting her part perfectly. This was the best training I could ever get.

"They... they're powerful." Lucia's hands shook by her side.

She was petrified of those who were running the slave ring. If she dared to say anything to us, they would probably hunt her down and kill her.

"We can help you. Please, let us-"

My hand was in my pocket, my dagger drawn before Justina had even finished the last part of her first sentence.

Lucia had moved her mouth, obviously whispering a spell. The others dropped to their knees. My heart beat in my head so loudly, I almost couldn't see. It was as if Lucia was making my eyes vibrate in my skull.

Her power hadn't quite got me as badly as last time. Which meant the warlock power in my dagger was filtering back into me. I was the only one able to bring her down. The others were in too much pain to do anything.

Seeing that I was still standing, albeit, only just, Lucia spun on her heel and started to run. My legs automatically followed her, my dagger in my hand as my arms pumped by my side. I would not let our only lead get away, if I could help it.

"Leave me alone!" Lucia shouted, throwing up her arm.

A kid's bicycle that had been laying on the side of the road came flying at me. I dodged it, swearing when the wheel missed my head by less than an inch. Okay, no more diplomacy.

The houses were still quiet as I raised my hand, envisioning a ball of flames. It formed instantly, the darker magic hot on my skin. Throwing it forward, I grunted as it left my palm.

"Shit!" Lucia yelled when it collided with her calf.

My feet slowed as she started to fall. And, yet, just as she was about to hit the ground, she propelled up, steady on her feet again. Little witch.

Huffing, I sped up, but it was too late. Lucia was obviously an Olympic runner, because her legs took her around the end of the road and out of sight. By the time another ball of magic was in my palm, she was gone.

"Devon, stop!" Justina's voice rang out behind me.

She wanted me to give up? No way. Although... My feet skidded to a halt, my leather boots scraping the ground. I had to listen to my boss. She was... well, the boss. It was tempting to defy her, but it would not help our already rocky relationship. Respect, Devon. I had to respect her wishes, even if they were diplomatic. Ugh.

Staring at the place where Lucia had disappeared, I got my breath back, waiting to compose myself before I faced the others.

"You just fired warlock magic at a witness. You're an idiot." Kurt clapped me on the back. "Shame it didn't stop her."

The man was an enigma. His bluntness, his praise. I never knew which one was good, which one was bad. But, I liked him. Not in a sexy way, I respected that he was Justina's man. Not only that, I had my own Dreamy Mac-annoying to content with. Not that anything was happening between us... yet.

"Diplomacy didn't work in this case," I said to Kurt, laughing along with him.

Justina approached, her eyebrows raised. Her body was clad in a leather suit, her big boobs not moving at all. Yes, that's how tight it was. Sometimes I wondered whether I'd pull off an outfit like that, but quickly realised that peeing must be a pain in the arse, so it put me off.

"Nice try," she said, pointing at a house. "Go search with Gerard."

Sighing, I dragged my feet as I did as I was told. Was she being sarcastic when she said nice try? Or, had she meant it? This job was so confusing at times.

Frustration ate at me as I headed for the open front door. Unspent magic sizzled in my veins, making me anxious. Pulling a ball into my hand, I launched it at the wall of the house. It exploded against the bricks, marking them red.

A smile came to my face as my energy balanced out again. It was nice to use my warlock magic again, but I had to be careful.

"Devon?" Kurt's voice was tense as he called me.

Turning, I frowned when my gaze landed on both of my bosses. They were rubbing their palms, a wince on their face. What was wrong with them?

"Something's... Do that again." Kurt's order was confusing.

"What?" I said, holding up my hand. "Throw another ball?"

Nodding, he gestured for me to do it. Shrugging, I did as he said, forming a bright pink magic ball this time. It was his colour; he could totally pull it off.

"Ouch!" Justina's cheeks turned red as she furiously rubbed her hand against her thigh.

"Great!" Kurt shouted. "The bitch has linked us!"

Huh?

"Agreed," Gerard shouted through the open door. "I just felt Devon's warlock magic filter through me."

Oh, that sounded... intimate. Which wouldn't have been a bad thing if the others weren't also feeling my magic. Ewwww!

"I don't understand. How are we linked?"

They both came to me, holding out their hands. Their palms were blistered, the skin puckered and red. Ah, okay, that was quite obvious. It was on their right hand, too. The hand I always used for warlock magic.

"I'm... Sorry?"

Justina shook her head. "Don't be, it's not your fault. Just don't use too much magic for the time being. Same goes for us."

My breath sucked in as someone else's magic wormed its way out of my fingertips. Wait, what was...?

"Gerard, you twat," Kurt called as I approached Lucia's house. "We're all linked. We can feel your magic, too."

Sticking his head out of the living room window, he grinned. "Sorry, I was just seeing if there was any paperwork that could link Lucia to her brother."

"Then search for it, like a proper detective." Justina shook her head, her smile only lasting a moment.

"Get back to work," Kurt told me, clearly wanting to speak to Justina alone as she turned.

Striding into the house, I joined Gerard as he searched through a desk in a small room. My hands instantly raked through a pile of beauty magazines that were sitting on an armchair. Even witches were obsessed with looks. Not me, though, I rarely brushed my hair, let alone put on tons of makeup. What was contouring, anyway?

"There's some photo's here, but…" Turning to face me, Gerard held up a picture of the witch we had just confronted.

"The head of the person she's with has been cut out."

Frowning, I snatched it from him, studying the mystery person's arm. A small tattoo was on her wrist where it rested over our new friend's shoulder. There was something about it…

"What do you see?" Gerard's breath fanned over my face.

I hadn't even noticed him move closer to look down at the picture. His energy was mixing with mine, the linking spell making sure that whatever happened to one of us, would happen to the other, too.

"I know that tattoo," I said, clearing my throat. "But, I can't remember why."

Footsteps sounded in the hallway as the others searched the rest of the house. If I could remember where I'd seen the tattoo of a pentagram wrapped in a rose vine and thorns, I might be able to pinpoint our suspect.

"We'll take these back to the agency. Maybe you can study them to help jog your memory."

Tucking them away, Gerard finished his inspection of the room. I followed, my brain trying to work. It was one of those memories that remained just out of reach.

"All clear," Justina announced as she came downstairs.

The house was spotless, unlike my apartment. The witch had pride in her home, which meant she wouldn't appreciate our grubby hands all over her stuff.

"Wait," Kurt said, pointing at the wall. "I've seen that before."

My gaze went to where he indicated a frame, hanging a little askew. No, no, no.

"Isn't that...?" Gerard's sentence fell flat as he snatched the spell off the wall.

Yes, it was another page from my mother's grimoire. How the hell was it in the home of a traitorous witch?

Reaching out for the frame, I frowned when my sweaty palms almost dropped the wooden surrounding. That made two of my ancestor's spells found in homes of those who were involved in the slave ring.

"I need to speak to the prisoners," I said, reading the top of the page.

It was a spell of protection. A simple, yet powerful spell. In fact, it was one of the first ever created by a witch.

"I'll take you," Justina said, waving Kurt and Gerard away when they went to protest.

Clinging to the frame, I moved to follow my boss. Instead of going outside, she paused, her hand on her hip. "We need to hurry this up."

Taking my wrist, she flashcd us. I gasped as my boots thumped on the concrete floor. The cells in front of me were closed off with individual doors. It was like a regular prison, except for the magic proof rooms.

"It's me," Justina announced when a guard got up from his seat.

Surely, she shouldn't have been able to flash straight into the supernatural jail? Unless she had very high clearance. I often forgot how kickass Justina was. She might be fairly laid back and low key, but her brain was always in gear. Whereas mine... the clutch of my brain had been burnt out long ago.

"Can you bring the prisoners to the interview room, one at a time?" Justina asked the guard.

Nodding, he went over to open the exit door for us. I studied the spell that was still in my hands as we went into a hallway full of doors. Interrogation rooms for all kinds of supernatural beings. Each one would be fully proofed to make sure none of them could escape or cause damage.

"Let me do the talking." Justina opened a door and ushered me inside.

Seriously? Why couldn't I beat their arses? I'd seen it in all the cop shows. And, those were human policemen. I should at least get a pass to get some answers. I could be the bad cop. It would suit my personality perfectly.

"Okay," I said, trying not to scowl down at the floor as I lowered myself into a chair.

"Don't sulk. If anything comes up that you think might help, you can talk. But let me take the lead."

A smile came to my face. I knew full well that something would come up, which meant, I was allowed to speak. As if I could just sit there with a straight face and not say a word. Did Justina know me at all?

"Here," the guard announced as he pulled a man into the room.

He was the witch that Gerard had shot at the hotel. When we had arrested them, they had come easily, unlike their much older lady friend. Her fight hadn't ended well for either of us. And, yet, we were all still here.

Slouching in the chair opposite us, the man, Harry, leant on his elbows. "It's you."

Instead of looking at Justina, like I expected him to, he was watching me. Errr, yeah, it was me. I had a memorable face, but his staring was a little creepy.

"Harry, we know that you're connected to the witch slave trade. If you give us a name, we'll go easy on you."

His scoff made me grit my teeth. The spell was on the floor, resting between my knees. I didn't want him to see it right away. There had to be a way to break his resolve, and if the spell was familiar to him, he would show us with his reaction when I revealed it.

"Are you not going to speak?" he asked me.

Sitting back in the plastic chair, I folded my arms over my chest. The press of my dagger into my side made me feel more confident. I had bought a light jacket with shorter sleeves to make it easier to carry my weapon. And, my phone, my keys... basically my whole life. It was much better than having a bag.

"No," Justina said. "Not yet, anyway."

The man had grey curly hair. It was short on his head, clipped low to reveal the growing wrinkles on his face. His build was average, yet, he stooped a little, his later years starting to catch up to him.

"I've already told you. We had a magic dealer, he-"

"A magic dealer? Like a drug dealer?" I snorted, unable to hold back my laugh. "Come on!"

Yes, people did deal in drugs, magic and slaves, but there was no way this guy was innocent. The magic that got people high wasn't as strong as the power the three witches had possessed. No, they had a much higher source.

Justina was staring at me, her eyebrows raised. She was lenient with me, I had to give her that. If it was the other way round, I would be pissed that she was laughing in the man's face. Although, if his expression was anything to go by, I had irritated him. Maybe I could be useful after all. Gerard often said that I was annoying. Maybe that would work in our favour.

"You know full well that I don't believe you." Justina leant over the table. "Which means you're probably going to be sentenced to death."

His eyes widened. Okay, Justina hadn't threatened that before. Good move, boss lady.

"The death sentence doesn't exist anymore." The man's hands shook slightly as he pulled them under the table to rest in his lap.

The handcuffs clattered on the surface, making me want to grab them to stop the noise. Metal scraping on anything wasn't exactly a pleasing sound to the ear.

Slanting her head to the side, Justina smiled. Her blonde hair almost touched the table as she drummed her fingertips on the cool surface. "The death sentence doesn't exist for humans anymore. However, it is well and truly in existence for supernaturals. How do you think the human government keeps us under control?"

The man's cheeks warmed to pink as he picked his fingernails. His gaze darted between us, his eyes blinking. Ah, nerves were a pain in the arse. But in this case, they weren't mine, so I didn't mind.

"Do you know anything about this spell?"

I picked up the frame and put it on the table.

His swallow answered me long before his mouth opened. Goody, he knew something.

"I... Where did you get that?"

Even more nerves as sweat lined the small space above his lip. I was enjoying the interrogation side of things. Maybe Justina would let me accompany her in more interviews. I could probably get quite good at scaring people.

"What do you know about it?" Justina pushed the question without answering his.

Rubbing a hand over his skull, he glanced between the pair of us. His brow furrowed as his gaze settled on me, studying every inch of my face.

"You don't know, do you?"

"Know what?" I snapped, ready to bring out my sexy little fists for a play.

If he didn't start answering questions, I would consider pounding them out of him. His smug expression would be too much if it wasn't wiped away. By me. And, my fists.

"That spell..." Harry sat back in his chair, his confidence apparently returned. "...It's from your mother's grimoire. I've got one at my private home. She... She gives them out to those of us in her circle."

"My mother is a part of the slave trade? No way! She's dead!"

His eyebrows rose this time, a small smile lighting his face. "I said... 'she' gives them out... I didn't say who 'she' was. You're going to have to torture me for that info. Or, kill me, I don't care."

11

My fingers shook as I picked up the envelope. It had been left in my letterbox in the hallway, but I had resisted reading it. The writing... it was way too familiar. And, not in the same way as my father's.

"Are you okay?" Gerard was outside the apartment entrance.

Tucking the letter into my pocket, I nodded and followed him to the car. Apparently, we were going on a little road trip. We had found the address to Harry's private home. And we were going to collect the spell he had spoken about.

"I'm surprised you've not offered to drive," my partner said as we both climbed in.

"On the motorway? You've got to be kidding me. Have you heard of the term woman driver? When it comes to motorways, I embody that term. However, any other type of driving, I'm amazing. So, don't be thinking you can be sexist with any remark about women drivers."

His smile would have usually lifted my mood, but the laugh that came out was forced. We both knew that I was pretending to be okay. When, really, the letter was burning a hole in my pocket.

"I got you a hot chocolate."

Handing me the takeaway coffee cup, he used his other hand to start the engine. I held the cup in front of me, frowning at it in a most intense fashion.

"How did you know I like hot chocolate?"

His laugh made my muscles finally relax. We were on duty. The letter would have to wait until later. I had to focus on the mission at hand. Harry had given us a clue about our criminal mastermind. She... was a she.

"Who doesn't like hot chocolate?" He winked as he steered the car into the flowing traffic. "Have you had any more thoughts on the tattoo from that photograph?"

Ah, yes, Lucia's picture had shown her with another woman. The head had been cut out, but her arm was clearly visible. The tattoo on her wrist had been a pentagram with roses and vines wrapped around it.

"No, I can't quite place where I've seen it before. Which is so frustrating. My memory is usually shit-hot."

Taking a sip of my drink as Gerard successfully navigated London's roads, I smiled to myself when the warm sweet liquid filtered down my throat.

"You look like you're enjoying that far too much." His glance was brief before he focused on the road again. "Maybe the tattoo doesn't mean anything personal. Maybe it's quite a common one."

Shaking my head, I closed my eyes and bought the image into my mind. A flash of someone kept trying to show, but I couldn't grasp them. "I... I think I've seen someone with that tattoo. It must be someone I was connected with because I get a bit of a heavy heart when I think of them."

"A heavy heart?" Gerard manoeuvred the car onto the entrance of the motorway. "You possess a heart?"

Ha bloody ha. He was in a sprightly mood considering we were all still linked. We had promised not to use our magic as much as possible. When one of us did, it drained the rest of us. And, we all knew how precarious my current magic situation was. So, of course, we had to be weak, because I was weak.

Ignoring him, I watched as we sped past the cars. Gerard put his foot down, his driving skills evident in the smooth way the vehicle took us to our destination. Was there nothing the man couldn't do? It was kinda hot. In an annoying way.

"The ringleader is a she... and she gives out pages of my mother's grimoire. How did she get the book?" I whispered to myself.

"I just assumed you had possession of it."

Coming off the motorway, Gerard checked the sat nav before settling into his seat even more.

"No, I've always had the one spell, but I don't remember ever having the book. I looked for it among my parents' stuff when Isaac Senior helped me box it up before I moved in with him."

"You lived with him?"

Checking the address we were heading to, I nodded without replying. A lump tried to force its way up my throat, but I wasn't going to let it get the better of me.

"We're here," Gerard announced, letting me off the hook.

There was no need to keep going over old ground. I had made a mistake. The biggest mistake of my life, and I had to live with that. It was time to accept it and move on. Especially now I was no longer the leader of the warlock coven. Although, they might seek to avenge their previous leader. Oh well, let them come.

The house we pulled up at was quite understated considering the opulence the three witches had lived in at the hotel. The man lived alone, according to him. And, yet, our weapons were within reach as we approached the cottage door.

Not bothering to knock, Gerard took something out of his pocket and started to pick the lock. I opened my mouth to speak, but before any words came out, a click resounded before the door swung open.

"Let's go," Gerard whispered.

It was pretty obvious that no one was there as soon as we walked in the door. Dust lined every surface in the hallway. Pretty antique furniture was starting to smell of mildew. What a waste. I could easily have the grandfather clock in my apartment somewhere. Maybe.

"Do you think he'd notice if I moved in?" I asked Gerard as we came into the living area.

We both stopped still as our gaze landed on the framed picture on the wall. The man had been telling the truth. Another spell was in the frame. Ripped from my mother's grimoire and handed to him as a prize.

Gerard went over and took it down, wiping the dust from the glass. It flew up into the air, making me cough. I thought my home was bad, my enemy had taken over as the winner of the dirtiest home award. And, I was happy to give it away.

"This is a healing spell. Again, same writing. Do you have any idea about your ancestry? Who wrote these spells?"

My mouth went dry at his question. If I pretended that my tongue was stuck to the roof of my mouth, maybe I wouldn't have to answer him.

"Devon...?"

He knew me too well already. Which sucked for me. I had been a pro at avoiding any type of interrogation before. Not anymore.

"Errr..." I slowly turned to check out the rest of the house, looking over my shoulder as I paused by the door. "Ever heard of the Essex witches?"

If I had my phone ready at that moment, I would've snapped a photo of Gerard's strong jaw almost dropping to the ground. Yeah, that nugget of information seemed to shock most witches.

"You're... an Essex witch?" He was frozen to the spot, his gaze glued to mine.

"Descended from them, yes. I don't think they actually exist anymore. My mum's line just happens to come from one of them. It's been quite a few hundred years since the witch trials."

A bang from the hallway made me shove my head around the living area door. I was about to throw my dagger when I paused.

"You would be an Essex witch if you were a full witch."

Okay. Why was Theresa, my former leader, in the house of our prisoner? Waving Gerard away when he went to storm forward, I stepped into the hallway.

"Your mother was an Essex witch, that's why she was treated with such respect. Her ancestors would've been furious that she married a warlock." The older woman's sigh made me clench my hands into fists.

"What are you doing here?" Gerard demanded as he came out of the living area. "This is private property."

His hand hovered by his side, his gun within easy reach. We hadn't come face to face with Theresa since Gerard had killed her best friend. A war was surely about to explode.

"I..." Theresa held up a hand and flicked it in a circle.

Gerard clutched his head as he fell to his knees. Only a coven leader would have the power to bring him to his knees. I wouldn't be able to down him with my magic, which meant I couldn't touch her.

"Leave him alone, or I'll use my warlock magic on you."

Swirling my fingers, I formed a ball of blue streams in my palm. Gerard rubbed his hand furiously as I raised my eyebrows at the coven leader.

"I'm not afraid of you. Your mother would've inherited the coven one day, but you're not her equal... yet."

"Yet?"

Theresa let go of the spell that was crippling Gerard. He shoved to his feet, glaring hard at our newest enemy. Our list was getting longer by the day. And, yet, I wouldn't give up the fight.

"You need to check that letter, Devon." Theresa put up a hand as I went to reply. "No, just read it."

My stomach churned. How the hell did she know about the letter in my pocket? She... she wasn't psychic. Unless...

"Did you write it?"

The handwriting was familiar to me. It was all over my mother's journals. The ones I had kept under lock and key since the day we packed them away. I couldn't bear to read about her life. But, my mother was dead. Theresa must have perfectly copied the way my mother wrote.

"What letter is she talking about?" Gerard asked as he shook himself from the effects of her spell.

My hand itched to reach into my pocket, but I couldn't read the letter with everyone staring at me. It was way too personal. And, none of their business either.

"You need to leave," I told Theresa.

The beat of my heart was slow and heavy. If she pushed me any further, there was a risk I would break. First I had received a letter from my dead father, and now, someone was playing a cruel trick on me.

"I can't."

Theresa stepped back when I rushed forward.

My boots thumped on the wooden flooring, pounding towards her. She raised her hands in surrender, her eyes widening as I drew closer. Before I reached her, I stalled, my hands clasped into fists at my side.

"Why are you here?" The words were bitten through my teeth. "Just to torment me?"

We had come to Harry's home to find the spell and any other clues leading to the witch slave trade. So far, we'd found the spell, but the interruption from Theresa was costing us valuable time.

"Not everything is about you," she said, reaching into her pocket.

Grabbing my dagger out, I extended it towards her. It burst into blue flames, the magic I had emptied into it igniting the blade.

"What...?" Theresa's eyes stared as she brought her phone out of her pocket.

"Devon, put it away."

Gerard's fingers took my free hand, shocking me back to reality. I shook the dagger, clearing the blade of the magic.

Shoving it into my jacket, I stared at the coven leader as she held out her phone.

Squeezing my fingers, Gerard let go and took it from her. His eyebrows furrowed as he read whatever was on it. "This is a report. Ten of your witches have been kidnapped in the last week?"

We both stared at Theresa when she nodded. "Yes, that's why I'm here. I know you're investigating the case. Devon, if you want to return to the coven, you can. I forgive you."

My teeth gritted together as I fought hard to control my temper. Gerard put his arm around my waist, bumping hips in the process. "She'll take it under consideration, won't you, Dev?"

"No I bloody well won't!"

If Gerard wasn't gripping my waist, my shaking body would be slamming into Theresa's. He was right to hold me back. I didn't want to hurt her. My actions would hurt me too. The fact that she could even dare to invite me back to the coven when she needed my help, after she had left me out on my own. It was just rude.

"You can hate me as much as you want. I don't exactly love you either considering how much stress your family has put me under.

143

But, I got a letter from your mother, demanding that I request your help. I... I thought she was dead, too." The hitch in her voice was real.

Rolling my eyes, I took a deep breath and shrugged Gerard off. I could hold on to my temper... as long as she didn't push my buttons any further. I wouldn't be held accountable for my actions if she dared to insult me or my family.

Theresa wrung her fingers together. "I missed her for so long. Resented her, too. For leaving me. For leaving you."

"Are you here because of my mother, or because you need help?" Her coven was probably always hit with the witch slave trade. And yet, she'd never reported it before.

"Both. Jeremy was holding back a lot of information from me. I found reports in his desk and on his computer. I didn't realise how many of our witches were going missing. I can't just allow it to happen. I'm prepared to do anything to help the agency."

Her sudden change of heart towards us was positive. It meant one less enemy to worry about. It also meant I could get close to those in her coven. Maybe one of them would know something.

"We're investigating the kidnappings. Do you know of a witch called Lucia Camos?"

Gerard glanced at me when I glared in his direction. Why was he giving her information? I hadn't told her that I'd help. I was just about to, but that didn't mean Good-looking Mac-butthead had to take the lead.

Theresa frowned, her gaze going distant. "No, I don't think so. I once knew a lady called Beatrice Camos. An Italian who approached me when she first arrived in London. She asked if she could join the coven, but as you know, we're pretty exclusive."

Yeah, so exclusive they wouldn't let me stay. Nasty people. But, then again, maybe I hadn't given them much reason to want to keep me.

"Well, thanks for the name," Gerard said, ushering Theresa out of the house. "We'll be in contact."

"You're dismissing me?" Her scoff of disbelief made me bite my lip.

Putting a hand on Gerard's arm, I almost jolted back when heat singed my fingers. His tattooed skin had given me an electric shock. I knew he was hot, but not that hot.

"Theresa," I said when he paused, "if you co-operate with the agency, including me, we'll help as much as we can. We're trying to save all witches."

Her gaze softened as she stared at me. Our history was wrought with disagreements, but she had been my mother's best friend.

"Read the letter, Devon."

Her last words repeated in my head as she allowed Gerard to escort her outside. She had obviously followed us somehow. Which meant we had been lax in our tracks.

Patting my pocket, I left the letter where it was and went to search Harry's house. There was no point in being in the bastard's home if we weren't going to check everything.

"She's..." Gerard stopped talking when he came into the office. "Devon... stay very still."

I had been reaching over to pick up the little bin beside the desk. My back froze, my arm still in mid-air. My breath rushed in as I tried to steady myself.

"What is it?" I couldn't exactly glance around to see what Gerard was looking at. "I know you're getting a good look at my behind right now, but if you don't speak up soon, I'll-"

"Be quiet! There's a spelled canvas right next to you."

A what? My head cocked to the side ever so slightly. My gaze was able to trace up the wall to see what Gerard was talking about.

Ah, yeah... that could be a danger. A painting of a wolf was attached to the terracotta coloured wall. Harmless enough. Until I spotted the wolf's eyes watching me like a bird of prey would its dinner. His tongue was hanging out, his breath huffing quietly. It was a guard dog, sort of.

"He's not ready to pounce yet, but it won't be long." Gerard's voice was calm, almost whispered.

The muscles supporting my spine screeched as I held my frame. Anyone who saw the painting would be wrong in thinking that the wolf in it was harmless. In fact, if he was triggered into believing that we were a threat, he would jump out of the picture, forming into his full size as he did. I had only seen it once before, when a group of teens, including me, broke into a well-known witch's house. It hadn't been a pretty ending.

"So... what do I do?" There was no time to be sarcastic.

Gerard's foot moved forward slightly, the wolf growled.

"He doesn't like you," I said, cringing as I held my calf muscles as tightly as I could.

If I wasn't careful, my super weak muscles would fail me, and I would fall on my face, probably evoking the wolf to attack.

Gerard's retreat made the wolf's face look a little less angry, if that could be possible. His growling stopped, and his tongue flicked to lick his nose. Or, maybe he was just getting ready to eat me.

Maybe, just maybe, the wolf hadn't pounced on me the whole time I'd been searching the office because he was alright with me.

"I'm going to try and move. I think he might like me."

A scoff came from the hallway. I ignored it as I slowly straightened my back, pausing every couple of seconds to check to see if the wolf had moved. Nope. Although he was staring at me, he wasn't panting or looking annoyed.

"See, buddy, I'm no threat. You're a handsome boy."

My teeth clenched when Gerard stepped into the room, and the wolf started to growl again.

"Get out," I said through my teeth.

He backtracked quickly. "Sorry, thought he had calmed down."

As the muscles in the wolf's hairy white face relaxed, I smiled to myself. "He didn't like you the first time, what made you think he would the second?"

A laugh rumbled from the hallway. I moved slowly as I rose to my full height. Something about the wolf was bugging me. Why wasn't he worried about me? I was an intruder. He should have jumped out and attacked me already.

Opening his mouth, the wolf panted as I took a slow step towards him. He was calm, watching me with those beady brown eyes. His head was 3D, as if it was sticking out of the painting now.

"What's going on?" Gerard's voice was strained, worried.

I stayed silent as I extended my hand towards the painting. Yes, I was crazy. But something about him made me feel safe.

"Devon?"

If Gerard didn't shut his mouth, I would be tempted to call him into the room, just to see his face when the wolf jumped out at him.

"Hello, there," I whispered when the wolf bowed his head.

My fingers brushed against the soft fur behind his ear. He rubbed against me, enjoying my touch. I had always loved animals, but this was...

"Are you crazy?!" Gerard exclaimed from the doorway.

My hand whipped back as the wolf's lip lifted and a deep sound came from him. I backtracked when its body pushed forward, its shoulders coming out of the painting.

"Devon, run!"

Finally listening to Gerard, I turned away from the now emerging wolf, ready to run. As I went to go through the door, I spotted something on the ground. An address book, lying on the wooden floor. Bending, I scooped it into my hand.

The thump of paws landing behind me made me squeak. No matter how much affection the wolf had shown me, I couldn't trust him not to hurt me.

A hand grabbed my arm as I ran through the doorway and into the hall. My heart leapt into my throat, pounding violently.

"This way!"

Propelling me before him, Gerard stayed behind me. Guarding me.

"Why did you do that?" I huffed as we ran through the kitchen.

The sound of nails on wood followed us. The quick movement of the wolf made my stomach flip. If he got Gerard, he would probably rip him to shreds. And, because he was a spelled picture, not a real wolf, Gerard couldn't use his magic on him.

"A door," I said, rushing towards it.

Trying to wrench it open, I swore when it didn't budge. Crap, it was locked.

A growl behind us made me freeze.

"Unlock it." Gerard's words were forced, tense.

Taking a deep breath, I focused on the earth beneath me and pulled on my witch magic. Muttering an unlocking spell, I almost celebrated when the lock clicked open.

"Hurry!"

I glanced behind me as I opened the door. The wolf threw its head back and howled before it looked forward. In a split second, it crouched on its haunches and pounced.

Shoving Gerard through the door in front of me, I spun just as the wolf was about to land. On me. Holding my arms up to cover my head, I screamed as my whole body shook. The wolf was going to kill me.

"Devon!" Gerard's scream mixed with mine.

And, yet... the pain didn't come.

A wind rushed around me, sending my hair spinning and covering my face. When I had shoved the dark strands out of my eyes, I froze. The wolf had come to a stop right in front of me. He was staring, his body shaking from the effort not to attack.

Fortunately for me, my partner had learnt his lesson. He stayed silent from wherever he was outside the house. He could probably see the wolf, watching me with his dark brown eyes. I had no idea what was happening, but for some reason, the magical creature didn't want to hurt me.

Taking a step back, I felt for the door. My hand brushed the wood as the wolf stayed where he was. I stumbled backwards, my heart thumping inside my chest so hard, I couldn't breathe.

"Thank you," I whispered as my feet somehow moved me out of the kitchen and onto the concrete patio.

The wolf stared, his eyes connected to mine. I released my breath when the door swung shut, blocking my view of something that I was sure to never forget.

"Are you okay?" Gerard was right there, his hands grabbing the top of my arms. "I thought he was going to kill you."

He looked down, his gaze checking me over for injuries. I shuddered as I broke out of the trance I had been in.

"I'm fine," I whispered.

Nodding once, Gerard let me go. Turning, he rushed away from the house. "We'd better get out of here in case it tries to come after us."

I stood still, my gaze following him as he went. He paused as he was about to round the corner of the house. There must have been something in the way I looked because he froze solid. Or, maybe the wolf was standing behind me, who knew. I was too dazed to focus much.

And, yet, we stood there, staring at each other. My heartbeat slowed, and my palms dried from the sweat that had lined them.

"See, everyone likes me," I quipped when I'd finally calmed enough to think normally.

One corner of his lips sunk into his cheek. "You keep telling yourself that."

"I will." Shaking myself, I went to him, a bounce in my step.

He didn't move when I came close to him, thinking he was going to start walking. My body almost collided with his as he watched me, his eyebrows drawn low.

"What is it?" I asked as I went to step back.

His hands grasped my wrists before I could move away. His intense stare made me shiver. That wasn't a look of lust, it was... penetrating. And, not in the feel good kind of way.

Air rushed out of his mouth and over my face as he heaved a sigh. I tried not to close my eyes as desire pulsed through me. It must have been the thrill of survival that made me feel that way. Serious Mac-intense was not the reason goose bumps popped up on every surface of my skin.

"Devon," he breathed, still frowning. "That wolf wouldn't harm you, which means only one thing."

It was my turn to screw my face up in confusion. "What?"

"Usually, the only reason any spell would be in alignment with you is because of DNA. The person who created the spelled picture, and namely the wolf, is probably related to you."

Related...? But, that was impossible... I...

Pulling my wrists out of his grip, I dug out the letter in my jacket pocket. Theresa had said that my mother had written to her. I had been in denial. My father's letter, now this one. It was impossible. They were dead.

"Read it." Gerard's strong but whispered words gave me the courage to rip open the envelope.

My breath sucked in as I saw my mother's handwriting sprawled across the page. It had always been a tad messy. She'd written me short stories as a child, telling me to keep my imagination alive. I still had them somewhere in my apartment.

"What does it say?"

The strength of his presence made me take a deep breath and read the letter out loud.

"Devon, I know it's been a long time, and for that, I'm deeply sorry. I cannot explain everything now, but I know you need our help. For too long witches have been kidnapped, and I can no longer stay in hiding. Your father and I wanted to protect you, so we left. It's a decision I will always regret. You see, we were in danger. We knew all about the witch slave trade, and we were working to bring the leader down. However, we could never quite catch up to them. When word got out about our extracurricular activities, we were targeted. I can't go into too

much detail, but we wanted to protect you, so we gave up our investigation and fled.

It's ironic that my contacts have told me that you're now working the same case. I'm proud of you, Devon. I never imaged my sensitive little girl would become an agent. We have much to discuss. I will be in contact again soon. Just know that you're not alone. You never were. I love you, Mum."

12

"**S**ensitive little girl?" Gerard scoffed as we jumped into a cab.

It was the night after the wolf incident, and we were on our way home from work. Justina had managed to pull some interesting contacts from the address book I had found. We were getting closer and closer to the big dog.

Laughing, I punched his arm as the door shut behind him. "Yeah, life has a habit of kicking that sensitivity out of you."

"Nah..." Gerard dug out his phone as it started to ring. "...there's still some sensitivity in there somewhere. I see it sometimes."

I was about to reply when my phone also burst into the stripper film theme tune. Justina.

"Looks like we have a job," Gerard said as he answered Kurt's call.

Swiping the green button, I greeted Justina. "What do you need?"

"Just had a phone call from your friend, Maxwell. He's uncovered a secret meeting happening tonight at a club in the East End. I'll text you the details and meet you there in an hour."

She hung up before I could reply. It was technically clocking off time, but we were never really free from our job. We had too much shit to uncover.

Gerard leant over and changed the address with the taxi driver. There was no point in rushing. We had an hour to get across town.

"Maxwell Maddocks. Seems he's finally on our side." Gerard lounged back in his seat.

My gaze roamed over his bare arms, the black and grey tattoos once again reminding me of his dark past.

"Seems that way," I muttered, leaning forward when I spotted something out of the ordinary.

Grabbing his strong forearm, I bent down for a closer look.

"Woah, Devon, I didn't think we were going there."

I bit my tongue as I glared up at him. Okay, so my head might have almost been in his lap, but his mind had taken it somewhere I had not been going. Although, now I was down here...

"What's this?"

I pointed at the small tattoo, tucked between the numbers. It was a distorted love heart with a crack down the middle. In fact, if I studied the tiny gaps between the bigger tattoos, there were several smaller ones. An infinity tattoo. A candle. Even two hands with fingers that were intertwined.

Gerard tried to tug his arm away, but I held firm. I wasn't going to let him get away with not telling me about these hidden tattoos. Everything on his body had meaning to him, he had made that clear.

"What are these?" I asked more gently as my finger traced the infinity pattern.

His breath sucked in as I glanced up at him through the hair that had fallen over my face. His eyes were wide, staring at me as if I'd asked him the most personal question in the world. There was no Mac-anything in

159

him right now, he was just purely Gerard. Open, vulnerable.

"Has no one ever noticed them before?"

He shook his head, his Adam's apple bobbing in his throat as he swallowed. My tongue flicked out to wet my dry lips. For some reason, his answer was important to me. I needed to know. And, yet, my insides churned at the idea of him opening up to me.

"No, you're the first to see them."

He tried to shift in his seat, but he didn't pull away. I looked down to see if there were more, to give him time to answer if he wanted to. My eyes spotted a star when his other hand reached out, the fingers gently holding my chin and turning my head to look at him.

He blinked fast as I straightened my back. We were close, looking at each other, but the energy flowing through us was more than sexual. It was openness, vulnerability.

"They're my hope tattoos. Every time something good happens in my life, I add another between the numbers. They balance me out. You see, I'm not all dark. I do believe that life hasn't given up on me. I just-"

"You need to stop adding the numbers," I blurted. "No amount of justice earned in this lifetime will save your soul. Only you can."

160

He frowned, his gaze turning hard. Before he could turn away from me, I grabbed the top of his very muscly arm and squeezed. "You have to forgive yourself, Gerard. That's the answer that you're looking for. If you can't forgive yourself in this life, you'll never know peace."

Clenching his jaw, Gerard stared at me, his eyes glaring into mine. Slowly, they started to soften as his tight jaw relaxed. "Maybe you're right," he whispered. "When I killed my best friend, his family blamed me for a while. Eventually, their anger subsided, and they accepted that it had been an awful accident. They forgave me. I still visit them now, once a month. My sister never blamed me. And, yet, I can't seem to..."

"Forgive yourself?" My soft words finished his dropped sentence.

The cab was taking us through London, but neither of us noticed. I had never seen Gerard quite so open, so willing to talk.

His nod was slow, his eyes looking down at his arms. His tattoos were suddenly sexier than before. The numbers were dark, the small ones in between light. The same contrast I had inside me. My warlock magic was dark, my witch magic was light.

Gerard looked into my eyes as the thought flicked through my mind. A smile came to his face at the same time as one came to mine.

"Will you tell me what some of the hope tattoos represent? Tell me the good things that you've experienced."

The smile fell from his face, but he didn't look away. He chewed on the inside of his cheek, obviously weighing up whether to give me what I wanted. What I needed. I had never thought about hope. I had never acknowledged when good things happened. It was natural to notice only the bad.

"This..." He looked down as he pointed at the broken heart. "...was my first girlfriend. The one where I was young and love meant something so different to what it really is."

That made me grin, his confession making my skin warm. His face had blossomed into animation as he remembered his first girlfriend. It was something so very different to what I was used to seeing.

"She broke my heart, but boy, it made me into a man."

Raising my eyebrows, I laughed when he realised his wording and rolled his eyes. "What about you? Who was your first love?"

The hilarity left me instantly. I sunk back against the seat, tempted not to answer him. But, I couldn't ignore him. He had just exposed himself to me.

"No one. I... I've never been in love, not really."

Glancing sideways, I tried not to cringe as he quickly changed his look of shock. What would he think of me now that he knew I had never experienced the most basic of human conditions?

"Does that mean you're a...?"

My mouth dropped open as I turned to glare at him. "Seriously, Nasty Mac-pighead? Is that your first thought? No! I'm not a virgin!"

He raised his hands in defence. "I'm sorry, that was very childish."

Huffing, I sat back, ignoring him when he chuckled to himself. We brought out different sides to each other often. Namely, me being a little brat, him being immature.

"Anyway, I suppose we better talk about Maxwell and the meeting."

I glanced at him, smiling gently to myself as he changed the subject. He'd had enough of sharing for one day. I didn't blame him, he had revealed a lot about himself.

"Yes. It looks like the witches and warlocks who want to create half-breeds are meeting tonight. I wonder if they're going to... you know."

I couldn't help it, my curiosity was burning. Would we walk into an orgy?

"I... erm..." Gerard stuttered. The thought obviously hadn't crossed his mind.

Trust me to be the one to think dirty this time. Not that he could blame me, he had been talking about my virginity only moments before. However, it was time to switch into professional mode.

"Either way, we need to see how Maxwell wants to handle it. It's his coven, we have no jurisdiction. He obviously wants our help to deal with it because it's illegal to inter-breed." I held up my hand when Gerard went to speak. "Yes, I'm a hypocrite. But, as you've seen, there's a very good reason it's illegal. I'm flawed."

"Fucked up, more like... in a good way!"

His insistence didn't help his cause. If he'd been wrong, I would've been offended, but he wasn't. If Becky didn't come up with a way for me to keep both my witch and warlock side, I would have to choose to be one or the other.

The cab pulled up at the end of a busy road. The nightlife was buzzing, the humans falling over in the street. Ah, the typical British summertime evening. Binge drinking, puking, and shagging whoever happened to be nearby at the time. It had never been my scene.

"Anyway," I said as we both climbed out. "How can a person be fucked up in a good way?"

Gerard's focus turned to Kurt's motorbike as it passed us. I followed his gaze as Justina followed behind on hers.

A deep feeling of excitement ran through me as the engine's vibration pounded through my body. "I need to get one of those. They're not sexy enough without me on it."

Ignoring me, Gerard marched towards where Kurt and Justina turned down an alleyway. I followed, my little legs only just keeping up. I would have to learn a spell to make my legs faster without me having to put too much effort in. My heartrate had not been healthy recently. Especially since all the stuff with my parents.

My footsteps slowed as an image of them came into my mind. They were alive. Or, probably... There was no actual proof. I had given my mother's letter to Justina but had swiftly tried to put it out of my mind. I had a list of growing things to think about. The ring leader of the witch slave trade, who was a woman, but that was all we knew. My powers, which were currently bubbling under the surface uncomfortably, even though I had drained some of my warlock magic before leaving the agency. The warlock and witch orgy about to go down. And now, my parents. How was I not having a nervous breakdown already?

"Devon, did you hear me?" Gerard asked as I walked straight into him.

"No, sorry."

Shaking myself, I closed my eyes and cleared my head. It was time to be the agent. Time to stop being distracted.

"I know you don't have to be told, but remember to keep your personal feelings out of this one."

The deep breath I took was because I needed to fill my lungs with air, not because I was going to punch Mister Mac-proper in the face. I had just told myself the exact same thing, I didn't need telling.

"So, if I don't need to be told, why-?"

"Devon, Gerard," Kurt luckily interrupted me. "Stop fawning over each other and get down here."

166

Our boss came to the rescue. If Kurt hadn't ordered us to hurry, I didn't know what would've come out of my mouth. Gerard had forgotten that I was speaking the moment Kurt had caught his attention. That was probably a good thing.

Coming out into the small courtyard behind the clubs, I waved at Maxwell who hurried out of the back entrance to one of them.

"Devon," he greeted, putting his arm around me.

I tried not to stiffen too much. We might have shared a ceremony together, but no touching had been required. It really should be the same now considering I was an agent.

"Okay, we don't have much time. They don't realise that I'm here. One of the twins tipped me off. He doesn't agree with what they're attempting to do, so he told me about this meeting."

Glancing at my three colleagues, I noted how each one of them listened to Maxwell intently. They were processing everything he said, waiting for the next bit of information. Not one of them showed any emotion.

"Okay," I said, taking a leaf out of their book. "Do you know how many are down there? And, the aim of the evening?"

Rubbing a hand over his tanned face, Maxwell cringed to himself. His purple suit stood out, even in the shadows of the courtyard. Whatever he was about to say was uncomfortable for him.

"They're going to... You know... breed." The last word was uttered with a shudder.

In any other circumstance, I would laugh at his prudishness, but not today. I knew the consequences of half-breed babies. I was one.

"So, we're going to stop them?" I asked Justina.

Her short blonde hair was tied up in a small ponytail, her body encased in her tight leathers. She nodded curtly, ready for business. We hadn't spent much time together recently, so it was good to be in the field with her.

"Yes, their plan is illegal. The government put Act 301 in place once they became aware of how powerful each supernatural group could become. It's one of their ways of keeping us under control."

I wrung my hands together as Kurt's gaze met mine. The implication that wasn't spoken rang out without a sound. And, yet, not one of them judged me. Not if their stoic expressions had anything to do with it.

It wasn't about me anyway. This was about the witches and warlocks about to commit a crime. It was my job to protect the supernatural world.

"Okay, there's two entrances. Maxwell, if you come with me and Devon, we'll head down to the basement. That is where they are, isn't it?"

Tipping his head, he gestured it downwards. I didn't know the layout of the club, so I would follow Maxwell with Justina.

"Kurt, Gerard, go around the front and enter from that side. Backup has just arrived so take them into the main club area. We can't have any suspicious activity above or those below will disperse. Once you've checked upstairs, join us in the basement."

Unclipping her gun from her waist belt, Justina nodded to each of us. We understood our mission. We would follow her lead.

Kurt grabbed my arm as the others moved away. "Don't let personal feelings about this situation cloud your judgement. I know how it feels to be on both sides. This is your biggest test, Devon. Fail it, and you'll be out of the agency."

He was about to move away when I stopped him with a hand on his chest.

Quickly pulling away when he looked down, I dropped my gaze. "How do you know how it feels?"

It wasn't exactly the time to be talking about the past, but I needed to know what he meant. If I wanted to pass the test, he had to help me understand.

Raising his hand, he held up a finger. I glanced around to see the others waiting for us. Oh great, had it looked like I was trying to feel him up? Surely they would know that I would never feel up someone else's man. Or, my boss. Or, Kurt. Eww, it was too weird.

"When Justina found me, I was torn between several groups. My ancestry is obviously based in witchery. But, I was adopted by a mixed coven of supernaturals. I lived among vampires, witches and shapeshifters. In the Australian outback. In a place that was very well hidden from the normal world."

My gasp was ignored as Kurt stared into the distance, his bright eyes dimming in the shadows. I had always wondered about him, and now I knew a tiny part of his history.

"This isn't the time to have this conversation, but eventually, the harmony that had reigned for so long, fell apart. And, I had no idea whose side I should have been on. Do you know the one side I didn't choose? The one side that should have been the most important?"

Shaking my head, I kept staring up at him. It was as if he had become more interesting than I had ever found him before. If he knew how I could disconnect from my emotions enough to do my job, he could help me become a better agent.

"Mine. I forgot about me. So, tonight, don't think about witches, or warlocks, think about your life, your job. What type of agent do you want to be? Harden yourself to others plights, or go home."

His last words hung in the air as he left me standing there. He had taken the time to tell me something personal, and yet, he didn't burst into emotion when he spoke about it. He owned himself. He knew who he was and why he was an agent, fighting the good fight.

Snapping out of my thoughts, I turned to follow Justina and Maxwell. I expected my boss to be angry, but instead she looked indifferent. Ready for action. I had to learn how to switch off enough to be like that.

"Right, let's go."

Her sharp words made me grab my dagger from the inside pocket of my jacket. The magic pulsed through me, trying to find its way back inside. Taking a deep breath, I forced it to stay in the dagger. My witch magic needed time to strengthen. I hadn't been practicing my spells much, so maybe tonight would be a good chance.

"Once we're down there, I will confront them," Maxwell said as he yanked open the back entrance door. "If they won't comply, I will leave it up to you to deal with them."

"Either way, they'll be arrested for conspiring to break the law. The government will need to know about this. If word gets out, the other groups might think of doing the same thing." Justina was matter of fact as Maxwell led us down a dingy corridor. It wasn't meant to be used as an entrance for guests, the peeling dirty white walls were disgusting.

"I don't understand their logic..." Maxwell sighed as he took us into the main wine bar. "...it's like breeding cats and dogs together. It just doesn't go."

I cracked a smile as the man who played the piano in the middle of the room caught my eye. He smiled back, not having a clue that I was laughing at Maxwell's absurd claim. And, yet, my fingers clenched a dagger that held the warlock magic that my body couldn't contain. He was technically right, supernaturals DNA just didn't connect well.

"Down here." Maxwell opened a door marked Private.

Scoping the room before I followed the others, I held back the longing to be normal. Humans were sitting at the bar, laughing and drinking their cocktails. Their elegant dress was accompanied by an air of sophistication that would never come with this job.

"Devon?" Justina called.

Going into the marbled hallway, I followed the pair to a door at the end. Maxwell paused, his thick fingers resting on the handle. The slight shake was testament to how nervous he was. I wasn't surprised. If I had still been leader, I wouldn't know exactly how to cope with what the people below were planning.

"It's time," Justina said. "Just walk confidently down the stairs and demand to know what's happening."

Straightening his purple suit jacket, Maxwell pulled the door open and marched down the steps. Justina followed, her gun held by her side. I was next, my dagger resting just behind my leg. I didn't want anyone to see it. If it burst into magical flames, it could cause some panic. Not only that, the warlocks who had raided my home had been aware of it, and they would be in attendance.

"What's going on here?" Maxwell's voice boomed.

As we stepped into the small room, the people scattered. There was a small bar along the far wall with a few round tables in the middle. The chandeliers were dim, setting the mood for a sexy evening.

"Freeze!" Justina held out her gun, her shout carrying across the area.

The same people we had seen at the meeting stopped in mid-movement. The creepy twins with their pale skin still sat at a table. One of them shrugged when the other whispered something. The ringleader, the tall black man who always wore a long coat, stepped forward, holding his hands up in surrender.

"Maxwell, it's a surprise to see you. What are you doing here?"

Oh, interesting. It seemed that the man might well plead ignorance. It was a good job I had heard his plan myself.

Maxwell pulled himself to his full height. His rotund stomach poked out from between the lapels of his jacket, but he stared the man down.

"Sit down," he ordered those who still stood.

They did as they were told, lowering themselves into the nearest chair. There were roughly ten of them altogether. Five witches, five warlocks.

"Why are you meeting with witches, Barry?"

It was interesting to see Maxwell act diplomatically. My own heart was beating in my throat, my skin tingling where my magic tried to push up through my body from the ground. And yet, I didn't want it. I wanted my pure witch magic.

Barry didn't sit down. He stayed standing, facing Maxwell. His long thin body was poised, ready to fight. And, yet, Maxwell remained calm, still.

"Are we not allowed to socialise with other beings?"

It seemed that Barry would play the innocence card. As far as I could see there was no evidence to prove what the group had been planning. There were no beds, no sex implements. In fact, it did just look like they were having a little get together.

"Is that the card you're going to play?"

Surveying the room as they spoke, I tightened my grip on the handle of my dagger when I caught sight of a curtained area at the back of the room. Now, that looked suspiciously like a bed could be behind it.

"What do you want me to say?" Barry held his arms to the side, his fingers moving slightly.

Maxwell threw up his hand, releasing a ball of dark blue magic. It puffed out in the air, right above Barry's head. The threat was real, but it had extinguished before it did any harm.

"I'm the leader of this coven, not you. If you don't tell me exactly what's going on here, I'll have you arrested by these agents."

One of the witches scoffed as she glared at me. "You have the cheek to berate what we're doing when you have her by your side."

Before another word could be spoken, Barry flung his arm, sending a stream of fiery red magic into the girl's chest. She jerked as if she'd been electrocuted and then fell forward, her head banging on the table.

Justina shot her gun in the air when a commotion broke out. Maxwell dove at Barry as he went to release more magic, wrestling the smaller man to the ground.

"Find evidence," Justina said to me as people slowed their movements, watching her.

They knew that if they went against an agent, they would be imprisoned indefinitely. And, bullets killed, even more accurately than magic most times.

Keeping an eye on the group as they sat in their seats again, I stalked backwards, my blade still clenched in my hand. The curtain was a light gold to match the walls of the bar.

"Get up!" Justina ordered Barry as he tried to crawl out from under Maxwell. "You're under arrest for the murder of that witch."

Well, at least Barry would be locked away for good. He had always given me the creeps, so that wasn't a bad thing.

My skin tingled as I reached my goal and flung the curtain back. The young teen who had been in my apartment with his dad was sitting on a sofa, a witch beside him. They were half dressed, their bodies completely still. They had obviously heard us enter the room and stopped what they were about to do.

"You're under arrest for the attempt to pro-create inter-breeds. You-"

A bang behind me made me spin. Fire was dispersing as Justina handcuffed Barry on the ground. A warlock legged it towards the door. It swung open just before he reached it, smacking him straight in the face.

Gerard and Kurt rushed in, their weapons drawn. They started to round people up, daring them to use magic. No one did.

My palms sweated as I glanced at the teen and his new friend. "Stay here. If you move, I'll use this on you."

Holding up my dagger, I smirked when the teen's eyes widened. He knew exactly what it was. The light blue flames that danced off it showed him that what he had been searching for was real. And, it was mine.

"The Essex dagger." The gasp came from the young witch.

Gritting my teeth, I indicated that she stay where she was. I couldn't think about her claim right now, I had to secure the area.

Maxwell called for silence, but hurried conversations and fizzing energy buzzed too loud in the air. They weren't going to back down without a fight.

"*Incendia!*" a witch shouted as she surged out of the group.

Fire ignited the curtains that hung near me. I jumped back, my arm outstretched.

178

Whispering an extinguishing spell, I heaved a sigh of relief when the fire puffed out.

Spinning, I joined the others in the main area. Gerard had caught the witch who had attempted to escape. Maxwell was on his feet, his arms in the air. The problem with warlock magic was that it was always physical, which meant there was no controlling an environment safely.

Coming in line with Gerard and Kurt as the witches and warlocks started to push and shove each other, I almost missed the slight movement behind the bar. I knew that hair. It was long, dark and lush.

"Lucia Camos!" I shouted to Gerard and Kurt, gesturing to her disappearing through a staff entrance.

"Go!" Kurt shouted.

I didn't need to be told twice. Our power had been halved because she'd linked us.

Darting across the floor, I jumped, vaulting over the bar. Wow, that was pretty...

"Ouch!"

Instead of landing on my feet on the other side, my arse hit the hard ground. Okay, my ninja move had failed slightly, but I was still over the bar.

Scrambling to my feet, I thrust through the door and followed the narrow corridor to an exit.

"You bitch!"

The shout came from Lucia as I slammed open the back door. It rebounded off the wall, almost knocking me back into the building. The exit led out to a side road. My target was disappearing down it, the dark almost swallowing her. My legs would have to pull out all the stops to catch up. I wasn't about to let her go.

Huffing in my breath, I ran as fast as I could. My muscles screamed at me as my arms pumped by my side to give me more momentum. My hair flew back from my face as I gripped my dagger in my hand. She was quick, too quick.

About to raise my hand to release warlock magic, I paused when the dagger lit up the way. It was full of magic. If I pulled more from the ground, I would be putting my witch magic at risk. I would be endangering my life. But, she was getting away.

Her laugh reached me as she gained a burst of speed. She was about to disappear down another street. I couldn't let her. Holding my arm high, I threw the dagger as hard as I could, praying to mother earth that I wouldn't kill her.

My breath stopped as the dagger spun with such force, it went flying straight into Lucia's shoulder. She fell to the ground, the force of the blow sending her crashing to the concrete. Okay, so I hadn't wanted to hurt the witch, but she was our biggest lead. She knew the leader of the slave trade, I was sure.

"That was cruel!" she spat as I came up to her.

The blade was lodged deep, blood seeping onto her pretty white top. The magic had gone, leaving the dagger a normal silver colour. Where had it...?

"I can't move!"

Ah, it had sunk into Lucia and paralysed her. Well, my magic was good enough to bring someone to their knees. Or, flat on their face in this case.

"Lucia Camos, you're under arrest for... many things."

I looked around for something to tie her arms with, just in case she regained feeling in her legs and decided to run. There was nothing around. The dark, quiet street was clean, unlike a lot of London.

Screwing up my face as I thought, I almost jumped out of my skin when a cat appeared out of nowhere. It made me think of Kingsley.

"No," Lucia cried. "Sammy, go home!"

My stomach churned as I watched the familiar cat come over to its witch counterpart. Justina would want to bring the cat with us. A familiar held a lot of a witch's power, just in case it was needed. In fact...

Swirling my hand in the air, I dragged warlock magic through my feet and into my hand, forming a line of glowing pink string. Bending down, I tied Lucia's hands behind her back. Her scream of pain from the blade still lodged in her shoulder didn't make me feel sorry for her.

"I'm sorry, but your cat wants to give you your power. And, I can't let it."

Going over to the approaching creature, I sunk to my knees, holding my fingers out to the cat so she could sniff me. She realised that I was no threat and rubbed herself against my hand.

"Please..." Lucia's plea was pathetic, but it hit me in the heart.

Kingsley was my best friend. For a long time, he was the only reason I still lived. I couldn't let Justina take the cat away.

"Lucia, you're going to prison." My flat statement made the witch sob.

I glanced over my shoulder to where she lay deadly still on the ground. A teardrop fell from the corner of her eye, tracing down her cheek and onto the cold hard concrete.

"Please, take her to my mother. Let her live."

A feeling of sadness crept into my chest as my phone started to ring. It was Kurt. Answering it, I picked up the cat.

"Are you alive?"

If I didn't have a moral dilemma waring in my mind, I might have laughed.

"I'm alive. So is Lucia, although she's currently..."

"Fucked!" Lucia's shout made Kurt chuckle.

Turning to my captured pray, I tilted my head to the side. "She's promised to tell us everything."

Lucia tried to shake her head, but I held up Sammy, her beautiful familiar. She quickly understood exactly what I'd do if she didn't comply.

"Good. Make sure she stays alive long enough for her to do that. Where are you? Justina and Gerard are cleaning up in here. There were some... casualties."

Clearing my throat, I cringed as the cat clawed my arm, ready to see its owner. I only just held on to her as I told Kurt where I was. Maybe I could sneak off just before he got there. He wouldn't understand why I had to protect the cat.

"Oh, and Kurt, when you say casualties, does that mean-?"

"Fatalities, Devon, yes." He hung up before I could reply.

Shit, what had happened when I left? If word got out that witches and warlocks were killed by the agency, it wouldn't be a pretty picture.

"So..." Lucia's face was still planted against the ground. "If I spill my guts to you lot, you'll take my cat to my mother? Is that what you're suggesting?"

Crouching next to her, I swore under my breath when the cat tried to get to my prisoner. "Yes. I understand what it's like to have a best friend."

Lucia's eyes blinked as tears clogged them. "Thank you."

Well, the witch had a heart after all. Maybe her information would finally lead us to the person we needed to catch.

Footsteps made me jump. Grabbing my dagger, I yanked it out of Lucia's shoulder.

She screamed as blood flowed from the wound. Kurt was a healer, he'd patch her up pretty quickly.

"I need to leave now if you want me to save Sammy."

The cat still clawed me, scratching my whole arm. Tucking my bloodied blade away, I backtracked away from Lucia.

"Devon?" Kurt arrived just before I could run. "What do you have there?"

Cuddling the cat to me, I watched Kurt over its head. His gaze narrowed on me, understanding crossing his face as he noticed the sobbing witch on the ground.

"Really?"

The harshness of his tone was countered by the wave of his hand. He had just given me permission to break agency rules. Yet again.

Instead of rushing off, I bit my lip as a lump came to my throat. I was about to speak when Lucia looked up at Kurt.

"Thank you," she whispered, saying everything I wanted to.

The mountain of a man ran a hand through his blond hair and stared at me. "If you don't go now, I'll stop you."

My hesitation was gone in an instant. I knew that he would keep his word. Which meant I had to hightail it out of there. The cat struggled as I ran away from the woman who might solve the biggest crime the Hunted Witch Agency had ever had to face.

But, at least the cat's life was saved. She might not ever see her owner again, but she would live.

13

"You agreed to take the linking spell off us." Justina paced.

Lucia was sitting at a metal table in the interrogation room. I stood on the other side of the mirrored glass with Gerard. My stomach churned with excitement as I watched my boss try to intimidate the prisoner.

"I did, and I will, once I've spoken to Devon."

Oh, I didn't see that one coming. If the silly witch said anything about what I'd done for her, I would probably get into a lot of trouble. In fact, they would probably fire me.

Justina waved a hand in the air. I glanced at Gerard, unsure of what she was doing.

"She wants you to go in," he said, grinning when my mouth dropped open.

"Really?" I couldn't help the hop that sprung from my feet as I moved to the door.

My partner shook his head when I threw a thumbs up in his direction. The fact that Justina was allowing me to enter the interview room meant that she must trust me. Maybe she wasn't as clever as I'd originally thought.

Kurt let me into the room, his expression a warning. He had also kept my little secret a secret. Which meant it was in everyone's interest to forget it ever happened.

"Devon, Lucia wants to speak to you." Justina lowered herself onto the chair opposite her.

Moving closer, I worked on my poker face. I would not let Lucia get the better of me. Even if she tried to...

"You wanted the truth, but I'm not sure you'll be able to handle it."

Her words made me almost frown as I sat next to my boss. I caught myself before the emotion showed on my face. What was she talking about?

"We know you're friends with the leader of the slave trade ring. Why are you protecting her?" I kept my hands folded on the table in front of me.

Lucia's eyes looked to the ceiling as she heaved air into her lungs. "These people are dangerous. You've seen my power. You know full well I'm connected to them. You found our..."

"Supply?" Justina spat. "We rescued them, you mean." Leaning forward, Justina slammed the metal surface of the table with her palm. "How could you use those witches for your own gain? Are you so weak and pathetic, you need to drain others of their power?"

I leant back in my chair, waiting for Lucia to answer. Nothing she said could justify her actions. She was a wicked witch. In fact, it was a shame she wasn't a warlock. The pure magic that they were using would be tainted by the way they were stealing it from others.

"They're a threat," Lucia bit between her teeth. "They will harm us in any way possible."

Erm... now I was confused. Who was a threat? Warlocks? The slave trade leaders? Nope, my brain had obviously switched off at the moment she thought she was making sense.

Justina cocked her head. "You really believe that getting rid of the warlocks will make witches lives easier? If that's the case, why were you at that underground orgy?"

My grin failed to stay hidden when Lucia choked on her reply. It was a shame she didn't choke for real, she kind of deserved it.

"I was there to spy for my friend. She knows everything. She takes most of the magic from the witches before she sells them on. You'll never beat her."

A part of me wanted Lucia to give me a good enough reason to forgive her. However, the more she spoke, the harder it was to feel any sympathy.

"We will," I said, sitting forward. "And, when we do, there'll be no trial. Only justice."

The energy in the room changed as Lucia slumped in her plastic chair. Her arms were still tied behind her back, but instead of my magic, handcuffs held her firm. Her dark smooth hair hung over her face as she breathed deeply.

"My brother got me involved with the group. I didn't want anything to do with it at first, but when he gave me extra magic, I was able to make a life for myself."

"How?" I was genuinely interested in how having extra magic made life easier. It certainly hadn't been the case for me.

As my question fell away, a huge burst of energy exploded from Lucia, the invisible bubble throwing us from our chairs. My back hit the mirror before my body slid to the ground, the air vanished from my lungs.

"That's how." Lucia's smirk made me clench my fist.

She was lucky we were in a safe place, or I would've gone for her. Kurt thrust the door open as I picked myself up from the floor. My jeans, which had already been ripped, were almost in shreds. But there were no marks on my skin. The bitch really had gone for it.

"Justina?" Kurt questioned his partner.

Scrambling up, Justina gestured for Kurt to leave before she brushed dust from her leather trousers. Her blonde hair was in disarray, the tips pointing out at all angles. Sitting back down, she indicated that I join her again.

I pointed at my hair, trying to let her know discreetly that hers was all over the place. Kurt was just leaving when he turned back around.

"Justina, your hair's shit. Sort it."

Ah, there was nothing like Kurt to make my world a brighter place. Not that Justina agreed if her scowl was anything to go by.

Ignoring his advice, Justina took a leather band out of her pocket and slapped it onto Lucia's wrist, above the handcuff. A magic diffuser might not completely stop her, but it would help.

Pulling away, she stared at Lucia, who wasn't actually basking in her glory. No, she looked sad. Was that possible?

An image of the young girl in the cinema a few weeks ago came into my mind.

"You're addicted, aren't you?"

What if I'd been addicted too? I had used my magic without thinking about the consequences. That had brought me to a place where I was lucky that I was still alive. Even now, the energy that bubbled inside me wanted an outlet. I had decided that I wanted to try and keep both types of magic, but was that actually doing me any good?

"Yes. Those that have access to the extra magic all eventually end up addicts. It's a big problem. One that I currently suffer from. One that Luis suffered from too."

Justina's fingers tightened on the metal, her knuckles going white with the strain.

She had a demon to exorcise when it came to that man.

"I know what he did to you." Our prisoner surprised us. "You were one of his first attempts at kidnapping. He had been groomed since we arrived in England. They trained him to need magic, to crave it. In turn, he kidnapped the witches who would be drained."

"And you just let him." Justina's harsh whisper made Lucia suck her bottom lip into her mouth, but she didn't answer. "You must personally know some of the witches who were taken."

Digging out her phone, Justina showed Lucia the picture of the witches we had found hooked up to the magic draining device. It was grim.

Looking away, Lucia held back a sob. "I don't agree with it, okay? I wasn't at that meeting to spy. I was there to try and help the warlocks. To have a baby."

"Are you crazy?" My outburst made them both look at me. Taking a deep breath, I pushed my emotions away, keeping as calm as possible. "You must have heard about me? I'm exactly what you were planning on creating. Trust me, I'm a mess."

Her scoff surprised me. "You're the crazy one for thinking so little of yourself. I've heard all about you. We all have. Some of the witches or warlocks who have seen you create magic speak about you being some kind of legend."

A legend? Well, if they insisted on-

"Trust me," Gerard's husky voice came over the intercom. "Devon is not a legend."

Trust Farty Mac-gravelly-voice to intervene in a very serious conversation. I was quite happy to hear exactly what people thought of me. It certainly was different to what I'd imagined. Although, I didn't care how anyone viewed me. Much.

"Let's get back to the two main points. You will unlink us right now." Justina leant over the table, staring straight into Lucia's eyes. "... And then you will tell us who this elusive leader is."

Lucia closed her eyes, whispered a spell, and grinned when both Justina and I gasped. A rush of energy raced through me, making me shudder. That would be the others magic unlinking from mine.

"There, it's done." Lucina had far too much power. The walls in the cell were supposed to stop anyone from doing magic. But, not her.

"Okay, you need to drain some of that magic." Justina looked at me, her eyebrows raised.

Was she talking about me? I had already sucked some of my warlock magic out of me. Why would I need to-?

"Give her your dagger."

My jaw almost hit the floor. She wanted me to give her my weapon? So she could put her filthy stolen magic in it?

"No. I've unlinked you. If you leave my magic alone, I'll tell you where the ring leader lives." Lucia's cuffed wrists squirmed in their bounds. She had used her inherited magic to make a point, but Justina hadn't done anything to punish her. My boss was too set on getting the information she needed. The magic would filter out of Lucia eventually anyway. Especially now she couldn't get another hit.

"Deal," Justina said, sitting back in her seat. "Go on."

The sadness in Lucia's eye made me question why she was upset. Was it because she was losing her extra magic? Or, did she genuinely feel guilty for the pain her people had been causing witches? Somehow, I doubted that.

"I'll write the address down. She's in Surrey, on the border of London. But, Devon..." Lucia paused as she blinked. "...I need to warn you, she looks scarily familiar to you. But with a million times more magic."

14

Justina was a bitch. Well, no, I didn't really mean that. However, she had refused to give us the name and address that Lucia had written down. I still had no idea who the leader of the cult slave trade was. And, apparently she looked like me. Lucky woman.

"It's so good not to feel your magic every time you grasp that dagger handle," Gerard said, winking at me when I scowled in his direction.

The van was going down a bumpy road, making my teeth rattle in my head. Another stake out. Another mansion. Couldn't one of them live in a proper run down house? One that would only take a minute to flush out.

The idea of searching through what felt like hundreds of rooms made me sleepy.

"You actually miss feeling me... erm... Wait, what...?"

My confusion was blindsided when Gerard knocked on the partition between us and the front of the van. Kurt slid the metal open, his rock music blaring through the gap.

"What?"

Ever since he'd told me about his childhood coven, I'd wanted to quiz him more on the subject. There hadn't been a moment spare to do that, so I sat on my questions, waiting for the perfect time to figure him out.

"I'm going to do what Justina suggested," Gerard said when Kurt turned his music down. "I just wanted to see if we had time."

Waving his hand, Kurt grunted. "Yeah, just do it."

The partition slammed shut before Gerard turned to me. He watched me from under his eyelashes. They were quite long against his grass green eyes. But, why was he looking at me as if he was... Was he...?

"I've noticed that you're weaker now we're unlinked."

"You have?" I almost choked at that.

I hadn't told anyone that I was feeling a little more tired than usual. In fact, I'd only

198

acknowledged it when I'd dragged myself out of bed that morning. I had to speak to Becky to sort out my magic problem. Especially now I didn't have three other witches as backup.

"I'm fine," I snapped, going to move to the end of the bench.

The van hit a pothole, making me bounce and thrust forward. Gerard steadied me by holding onto my knees. He stared at me, a question in his gaze. We had been so engrossed in the unfolding drama, we hadn't spoken about anything else.

"You're not fine. I can feel the struggle within you."

My chest squeezed, the air rushing from my lungs. I had pushed my own problems aside, trying to be professional. I hadn't been an agent for long, I still needed to prove myself to Justina.

"This isn't the time," I said to him as I tried to shove his hands off me.

It didn't work. He held tight, still keeping his intense gaze trained on me. Ugh. If he was going to get all protective, I might as well get it over and done with.

"So, what did Justina suggest you do? Lecture me? Give me therapy?"

My indifference was met with a quirk of the lip. "I'm always lecturing you, so no, not today. However, I'm going to give you some of my magic. Your witch side is still compromised, and if this battle is going to be won, we need you at your best."

"You don't need me," I blurted before I had a chance to think.

Great, well done, Devon. Tell the man your insecurities and make yourself look like an immature fool. Ugh. Why was I so...?

"What makes you think that? You're the first partner I've ever had that has kept me on my toes. You might have brought a lot of the crap with you, but hey... it's been fun, hasn't it?"

Gerard's jovial mood turned serious when Kurt banged on the partition to tell us that we had ten minutes until we got to the house. My heart flipped in my chest at the thought of finally catching our target.

"Let me give you some of my magic. Please."

I closed my eyes. The string of magic that was pure was a hell of a lot weaker than my warlock tie to the earth.

"Okay. But, maybe I need to seriously start thinking about being a warlock. The magic. It seems to want me to use it." My words were uttered with a sigh.

I didn't feel sorry for myself, just resigned. There was a reason the warlock side of me was stronger. Maybe my witch magic should be severed. It would make life a lot easier. And me a lot stronger.

Holding out his hands, Gerard looked into my eyes. I placed my palms against his, my heart aching slightly as his warm energy filtered into me. My mouth parted slightly as I inhaled, my chest rising. Gerard's eyes followed the gesture. Sharing something so intimate just before a raid was a questionable idea. Especially as it made me want to rip off his jeans and tight jacket. The weapons would go sprawling as I jumped on him...

"I don't want to know what you're thinking." Gerard's voice was deep, husky.

My eyelids were heavy as his magic poured into me. Oh, man, maybe it wasn't such a good idea. I might not be able to control myself when I watched Sexy Mac-horny fighting, his muscles bulging.

"No, you don't." My whispered words made his eyebrows raise and his cheeks flush pink.

Releasing my hands, he clenched his jaw as he sat back. "That was intense."

"Thank you."

Yes, it was lame, but it was the only thing I could say. My stomach was home to a party of butterflies, making me feel a little nauseous. We had been so focused on our mission, we hadn't had a chance to acknowledge that the attraction still existed between us.

The van slowed to a stop. Gerard leant forward, his arm reaching to grab my chin. I tried not to cringe as he pinched the skin slightly. "Be careful."

He was out of the van before I could react. Be careful. Pfft. I didn't need to be careful. I was Devon Jinx. Half witch, half warlock. For now.

Glancing down at the floor, I smiled when my gaze caught my boots. The laces were tied tight, ready for action. Like me. Although, not that kind of action. Not right now, anyway.

"Let's go!" Kurt slapped the side of the van, rattling the metal. Grabbing out my dagger, I hopped down onto the ground, swearing when I landed straight in a muddy puddle, the dirt flicking up all over me.

"Classy, Devon," Justina quipped as she shone a torchlight on me.

A laugh escaped her as my black leggings and khaki jacket were revealed to sport a new style of blotchy mud.

"Its fine, I'll blend into the bushes."

Kurt's cough alerted me to his presence as he pointed to our right. I came around the van to get a look. A field stretched ahead of us, leading up to... was that...?

"Is that a fucking castle?" I exclaimed.

The others stared at me. The high walls made of stone were a pretty obvious giveaway. How the hell were we supposed to get into it?

"Didn't you get the memo?" Justina asked as she clipped a gun to her waist belt.

Memo? Since when did we get memos? Okay, if I would have known we were going to be scaling some walls, I would've done some push ups before we came.

"Do you ever check your phone when it doesn't ring?" The glint in Justina's eye promised me that she wasn't about to fire me on the spot.

"What... emails and stuff? No. I check Facebook and Twitter sometimes, but never my email."

"Sometimes?" Gerard scoffed. "You're addicted to Facebook. You literally check your witch group every hour. Just in case someone has said something about you."

My secret obsession with social media obviously hadn't gone unnoticed. Not that I flaunted it that much, so I didn't know what Gerard was talking about.

"Focus." Kurt snapped his fingers in front of my face.

Instead of throwing the blame on my partner, I stiffened my back and waited for my orders. I was full of both witch and warlock magic, with a little extra warlock in the dagger if needed. It was time to bring the bitch down.

"Devon, Gerard, head across the field and see what protection they have. There will be a barrier spell. There might even be physical security too. We'll stay in the woods and approach the front entrance. I checked on the maps, but I didn't realise how big a fortress it was until I used the government's equipment. We won't be going in today." Justina handed Gerard a walkie talkie.

My skin itched as frustration ran through me. Ah, crap. If only I'd read the memo, I would've known that I wasn't going to get my magic on.

"Got it?" Kurt checked in with us both, his eyes narrowing on me.

"Did I lose it the other night?" I said, trying hard not to sound sarcastic and failing.

"No, but there's no harm in a little reminder. You're bloody unpredictable."

My male boss still didn't trust me, which sucked. I probably hadn't given him cause to considering I'd broken the rules a few times. It had got results though, hadn't it?

"Okay, kids." Justina interrupted the glare that Kurt and I shared. "Shall we be adults now? And, get on with our job? Please?"

Checking my dagger was in place, I saluted Justina and turned with Gerard. My eyes landed on a wooden stile. Oh great, my gorgeous leather boots would have to traipse through mud.

"Report back every five minutes." Justina's parting words were accompanied by a wave of her hand.

Gesturing for me to go first as the others disappeared, Gerard stepped back. Hopping over the stile, I smiled to myself when I landed on hard ground. Good, it hadn't rained enough recently for the squelch to have got the ground.

Surveying the dark field, I made sure there were no lights or suspicious activity. My eyes were now used to the dark, adjusted to see anything out of the ordinary. However, I wasn't a rabbit, I couldn't see completely. We would have to tread carefully.

"This is a bit dodgy," I said when Gerard was next to me.

We aimed towards our goal, the big double metal gate at the bottom of the field. It was visible in the slight moonlight. On the other side, the grounds led to the castle. The walls weren't that high, the castle only being a small battlement. There was no moat or big turrets, just a smaller place with tons of land.

"There's lights on in those tiny windows," I said, almost excited that we were approaching a historic building.

Gerard's grunt alerted me to his concentration. The grass tufts made it harder to keep a steady step. However, we had to be quiet. Oh, yeah.

Pretending to zip my mouth shut, just as my own reminder, I concentrated on where I was stepping. We had to be as quiet as possible, which was kind of impossible for me. Especially when my foot caught, and I toppled over.

Rough hands grabbed me up, hauling me to my feet. Okay, Rough Mac-handly, no need to put your hands-

"Ah!" I exclaimed when I slipped again, and Gerard's hand accidentally brushed against my arse. "Right, let me get my bearings."

Stepping away from him, I stopped for a second. He hadn't said a word, but my cheeks burned anyway. We might have shared a kiss, but touching body parts wasn't currently on the cards. Unfortunately.

His chuckle rent the silence, making me grit my teeth. It wasn't the time to be humorous about my arse.

Clearing his throat, Gerard came a little closer and whispered. "We don't have all day. Do you want me to carry you?"

I batted his offered hand away, pleased that I couldn't see the expression on his face. His shadow loomed over me, reminding me that I was tiny in the big scary world.

"Pack it in. I'm ready to get on with it." My hiss was acknowledged with a nod of his silhouetted head.

Straightening my jacket at the same time as patting my pocket, I reassured myself that I still had my weapon. Bending my knees as I walked, I gained a better balance in the ruts.

The gate loomed ahead as we neared. No one was in sight, which made me nervous. My stomach fluttered as I came close to the edge of the field. If this was the fortress of the leader of the slave trade, there would be some-

"Wait!" Gerard hissed when I went to reach out.

Holding my arm frozen in mid-air, I waited for him to join me. He pointed to some wooden posts that held the metal gate. I squinted, but he must have had amazing eyesight, because they just looked like dark wood posts to me.

"They're burnt," he said, shining a tiny light onto one of them for a slit second. "Which means the barrier spell might be..."

"Electric," I finished for him when my foot trod on something that wasn't the ground.

I jumped back when I looked down and saw an array of shadowed furry lumps. Animals that had been shocked to death. A lump rose to my throat as I stared, unable to stop the images that were running through my mind. What was it with the brain and morbid curiosity? Why was I now imagining tons of poor little creatures frying from electric volts?

"We need to disarm it if we want to get any further. However, they might have an alarm system in place." I was speaking to myself, trying to forget the dead animals on the floor.

A click made me look at Gerard's shadow. He was extending something towards the gate. Was he going to interrupt the spell?

Nothing happened. And, yet, he stayed completely still. Er. What was he doing?

"Gerard?" I came a little closer to him. "What...?"

The small blast of flames that came from his hand made me step back, almost tripping over, yet again.

"Keep your voice down. That was a test, which might have triggered a warning, so we need to be on the lookout.... and ready to leg it."

The walkie talkie buzzed, Justina's whispered voice coming through. "The barrier spell is strong at the gate. How is it there?"

Handing me something, I stared as I tried to work out if it was the thing he'd just used or...

"Hello?"

I almost dropped the dam walkie talkie when Justina's voice echoed in my hands. Okay, he wanted me to talk to her.

Pressing the button, I spoke back to my boss, trying to keep my voice low. "It's covering the gate and tree line here, too. Gerard just did something funky. Flames erupted, not a lot else happened. Quite anti-climactic actually."

Justina whispered something on the other line. Obviously telling Kurt about our failure at getting very far.

"Did he not explain that he was pushing the spell with a device that is scientific? No magic involved? I see he's doing a great job at training you."

The accused grunted as he took something else out of his Mary Poppins jacket and brought it to his face.

"He's putting on a mask or something now. I have no idea what's going on."

Snatching the talky out of my hand, he moved closer to the gate. "Justina. I didn't seem to set off any alarms, although I'm not certain on that one yet. However, I've just used the binoculars, and I can see thermal images of supernaturals just outside the walls of the castle."

"Yes, we can see them here too. We've got vampires."

What? My jaw dropped open when Gerard hummed an affirmation. "I've got shapeshifters. We need to be very careful."

His voice had lowered considerably. How had they not heard us? My skin warmed, the tightness of my jacket pulling on me. Oh, had Gerard covered us with a spell? And, I hadn't even realised? Great job, Devon.

Not only had Gerard given me some of his pure magic, he'd placed an invisibility spell on me too. Without my permission. Although, it was hard to be mad at him considering I should have noticed instantly. Which I would've done if I hadn't been playing magical footsies.

"Check the boundary, see how far it goes."

Gerard's confirmation was followed by him passing me the special goggles. I looked through them to check the thermal images. My heart leapt into my throat.

"Er… Gerard, you know you said that the test didn't get their attention? I think you might be wrong."

I had already started to backtrack, my feet tripping over the mounds of grass and animals.

Taking the glasses back, Gerard looked through them, swearing when he saw the advance of three people. Spinning, I started to run across the field. My feet slowed when I didn't hear footsteps or puffing beside me.

Looking over my shoulder, I almost tripped when I saw Gerard bending down by the gate. Did he have a plan that I didn't know about? I somehow doubted that the element of surprise would work in this case. Idiot.

I was about to head back when he shot up from his crouch and sprinted towards me. Thank goodness. I wasn't in the mood to rescue my partner from shapeshifters who were working for a crazy witch.

Adrenaline thumped through my veins as my muscles moved. My feet were slippery on the grass, my boots useless against the smooth damp surface.

"Devon, I've left them a little treat. It might be a bit risky, but I think..."

When the explosion rocked through the air, Gerard was cut off. We were thrown forward, the force of the magical blast sending me flying. My hands just about caught my body on the ground as my wrists screamed out in pain.

"What the hell were you thinking?" I shouted, seriously peeved that he had blown our cover even more than was necessary.

"What the fuck is going on?" The walkie talkie burst into noise. Justina didn't sound so diplomatic now.

The sound rattled in my ear. Gerard had obviously dropped the bloody thing. Snatching it up, I pressed the button as I climbed to my feet.

"Gerard decided to blow a hole in their barrier spell."

My breath rushed out of me as something heavy landed on my back, sending me sprawling to the ground again. Ah, shit, the shapeshifters. The claws of the animal sunk into my skin, making me shout out a nasty swearword. My mother would have killed me if she had heard me call him a-

"Devon!" Gerard's voice was nearby.

The heaviness lifted from my back, allowing me to spin and jump to my feet. The wolf... yes, how ironic... was wrestling with Gerard. Its light fur was visible in the moonlight.

Checking around for any sign of another threat, I winced when the wolf head-butted Gerard. Ouch, that had to have hurt.

It looked like a couple more shifters were in the middle of the next field, coming towards us from the castle. For some reason, they hadn't shifted yet.

"Devon!" Gerard's call of anguish made me whip out the dagger.

The muscles in my arms were stiff as I held it high in the air. Gerard's arms were straining where he was holding the wolf's neck away from him as it gnashed its teeth towards his throat. If I didn't do something soon, he would be killed.

"I'm sorry," I whispered as I crouched.

My warlock magic surged through me, a line of blue fire extending from the palm of my hand and shooting over the blade as I plunged it into the wolf's throat, ripping the skin. It froze, blood pouring from the wound. Gerard shoved it off him as soon as it went limp.

His feet were speedy as he scrambled to stand. Tugging me, he dragged me across the rest of the field before the rest of the shifters could join us. Hopefully they wouldn't be able to see us in the dark.

"You're covered in blood." I huffed as I ran alongside him, somehow keeping my footing.

The stile came into view. Oh great, knowing my luck, I'd-

A hand came round my waist as I reached it, pushing me up and onto the wooden step. I vaulted over the rest, grateful for Gerard's help.

"Run!" Hopping over the stile himself, Gerard turned to check the field.

Throwing his hands in the air, he muttered a spell. He'd used one of my mother's powerful protection spells. Where had he got that from?

The sound of the van's engine brought a sigh of relief with my puffing breath. Gerard shoved me from behind, making me move faster as Kurt pulled up in front of us.

"Get in." His demand was stony, angry.

At least it wasn't my fault this time. Gerard would have to take the blame. He was the one who decided to draw attention to us. Which was something that wouldn't help our cause in the long run.

He wrenched open the door before I got there. I leapt in, knocking away his hands when he tried to help me again. It was a rash action, borne from frustration.

"Okay," Gerard shouted as he slammed the door shut behind him.

There was no need for him to say anything, Kurt was already speeding down the bumpy track. My stomach rolled as I bent over, grabbed a random box from the floor and heaved up the contents of my tummy.

"Are you okay?"

215

Glancing up at him, I raised my eyebrows. The red splash of blood was all over his face. He grabbed a grey towel from under his seat and rubbed it over his head. I swallowed back the next threat of bile and threw the box out of the window to get rid of the smell.

"I..." Clenching my fists, I stared at him. "Why did you do that?"

He shook his head, his hands held up in surrender. "You think I did that on purpose?"

Huh? Didn't Stupid Mac-crazy not understand what had just happened? He had exposed us to the risk of being caught by the slave trade ring leaders. The people we had been after all along.

"A magical bomb going off after you were crouching by the gate might have given me a clue! You mentioned you'd left them a gift."

His shake of the head sent a drop of blood flying onto my blue jeans. He quickly wiped it off, his eyes going wide when he looked at me.

"That bomb was already there. It was a protection mechanism. I saw it before we were about to leave. I was trying to disarm it, but I couldn't, so I let it explode, hoping it would slow them down."

His green eyes watched me from a face still splattered with blood. He looked so sad that I had accused him of ruining our mission. I couldn't stay angry at him.

"I'm sorry, I..." Running my hands through my hair, I struggled to look at him. "...I thought you'd..."

A smile came to his face as he sat forward. "Justina's right, I'm not training you very well. Do you not trust me?"

"I don't trust anyone," I blurted before I could think. "I mean..."

His lips pursed as he gave up trying to get rid of the blood that covered him. Blood from a wolf. Blood from a shapeshifter.

"I killed a man," I whispered, my eyes tearing up without my consent.

Blinking rapidly, I grabbed the bench as the van lurched onto smoother ground. We were back on the road to London.

"You've killed before." Gerard's statement made my heart slice in two.

Yes, I had killed my guardian. But, I hadn't been in control when that had happened. I'd also been using a gun. I'd never actually used a blade full of my magic to disarm and kill a person. Ever.

It wasn't something I wanted to get used to, no matter how much I wanted to be an agent.

15

"They're coming here for a meeting now," Justina announced as she came into the library.

Most of my missions had been out in the field so far. Justina's cosy office was one of my favourite places in the agency. I missed it when I wasn't here. The leather chair that almost hugged me made me feel safe.

"The vampire leader?" Lilia squeaked, reaching for Kingsley.

I'd had to bring my pet rat to see the witch I rescued for a visit. Every week. She had looked after him when my home had been ransacked. And, now, apparently, they'd become best buds. Well, thanks for nothing, Kingsley.

My finger reached out to stroke the grey fur that lined his medium sized body. He was my little boy, meant to be my familiar. I still couldn't bring myself to link with him. I didn't want him to support me that way. He would be in even more danger than he was now. Not only that, I was still paranoid that my split magic might do him harm.

"Yes, the vampire leader, Antonia, and the shapeshifter leader. Apparently, she's bringing him with her. I've never met him before so I have no idea who he is. In fact, no one does."

Lilia got up from her seat, handing me Kingsley as she did. The rat tucked himself between my shoulder and neck, his whiskers tickling my skin.

"I better get on with my work."

Justina nodded, indicating that she could leave. My boss had taken Lilia on as an administrator, allowing her to live in the agency building. The witch was slowly regaining her powers after years of being drained for someone else's use. The witches we had rescued from Luis Camos were recovering quickly, most of them moving away to rebuild their lives. We had got all the evidence we could from them, but like Lilia, their memories had been mostly wiped from their mind.

"Devon, you know both Antonia and Kalic." Kurt paced in front of the screen of security cameras. They covered the whole of London, piggy-backing off the government's systems. "Use that to our advantage. We need them to co-operate."

Nodding once, I eyed Gerard when he came in the door. His footsteps were heavy, his leather boots slamming on the wooden floor. A scowl was on his face as he lowered himself into a chair.

"Gerard, this isn't the time to be-" Justina started.

"I'm fine," he snapped back, his gaze avoiding everyone in the room.

It had been a while since I'd seen Gerard in one of his moods. With us being so close to our goal, he seemed to be quite cheerful, if I could actually call it that.

"Go back out the door," Kurt said. "And, leave it outside."

Closing his eyes, Gerard got to his feet and did as he was asked, no questions. Our bosses knew us better than most people. I might not have been working there long, but they'd been studying me for a while. They knew what made me tick, what made me hurt.

"The letters your parents sent you," Justina said, cutting into my thoughts. "They're authentic."

Before I could react, Kurt lowered himself onto the arm of my chair. His hand clasped my shoulder, offering me his version of support.

"The reason we're telling you this right now is because we also got a letter from your mother just before we went on the raid last night. She gave us the same address that Lucia did. It said that she had to stay in hiding."

My heart was fluttering, but I kept my cool. So, my parents really were alive. And, they had abandoned me. Great.

"When I ran away from my coven, I left people behind. Vampires, shapeshifters and witches. They resented me for years. Until I went back five years ago." Kurt lifted his hand from my shoulder. "They almost killed me when I walked in. The coven might have self-combusted, but there were still people left. People who had loved and trusted me. The vampires shunned me for a long time, but the witches let me train with them again. I learnt more the second time I was there, using herbology to help them heal some of those who had been permanently injured in the fights before I left. They realised that I hadn't abandoned them. I'd saved myself. I was a target because I had no family, and yet, I was very powerful. I was a top, well respected witch at the age of twenty. They felt threatened."

"So, you left others behind to protect yourself?" My words could have been blamed on the anger that simmered in my veins. It was as if he was telling me his life story to excuse my parents.

Glancing at Justina as she came over, he smiled gently. "No, I left them behind so they weren't killed because of me. The vampires were slaying those associated with me because I was pushing the boundaries of magic. They didn't like it. If witches became too powerful, they would tip the balance in the coven."

Staying quiet, I thought about what he'd said. He was trying to explain that my parents may have left to protect me from danger. Maybe they had.

"We've dug up some of your history. I want you to know some of it because it's common knowledge in the circle of supernatural group leaders." Justina handed me her tablet.

Several pictures of grimoires and pages ripped from them were staring up at me. My eyebrows creased as I scrolled through, trying to read the smaller writing.

"You're an Essex witch." Justina sat in the chair next to me.

"I'm from a line of Essex's witches, but it's..." My mind went blank as I tried to recall the history my mother had taught me.

Taking the tablet from me, Justina flicked to a grainy picture of a grimoire. "This was taken in 1884. By your great, great grandmother. She was a full Essex witch, and so was your mother."

An Essex witch? They were extinct, or at the very least, watered down. I'd heard my mother speak to Theresa about her linage, but I was sure it wasn't a massive deal. I knew the coven treated her differently because of her ancestry, but... surely, she couldn't be...?

"There are four surviving Essex lines. Your grandparents were from two of them. When your mother broke the sacred pact of keeping within the four families, she was disgraced." Reaching out, Justina took my hand. She kept her gaze on mine, making sure I was listening. "You still have Essex blood running through you, even though you're also a warlock. You... you're one of kind, Devon. Your mother ended her Essex line when she married your father."

"So, that's another reason she ran away?" I didn't know how I knew that, but it would make sense.

My parents were always regarded as outcasts. Now I knew the extent of their scandal. No wonder the witch world were against the match. Not only was it against common law, my mother had broken a tradition that kept the Essex witches alive.

The door opened and Gerard came in, bringing me back to the present. His frown had lifted and his energy lightened slightly, although something still bothered him.

"They're at the front door," he said, aiming his words towards Justina.

Kurt stood, leaving me to stare after him as he went to greet our guests. Justina moved to her desk, gesturing for us to join her in the seats she'd pulled around to her side. She wanted our backup. No wonder, considering what we were about to ask of the leaders.

"Is everything okay?" she asked Gerard.

225

Clearing his throat, he glanced at me before nodding once. "Sorry about that, my sister rang me this morning. She wants to move away, that's all."

"Okay, let's talk about it after this meeting. I want your mind in the game now." Justina tucked her short blonde hair behind her ear and sat straight in her chair.

The door opened. Kurt led the way, followed by Antonia, a man with Asian features, and Kalic. Antonia was wearing an old fashioned steampunk dress, her dark hair up in a high ponytail. I hadn't ever seen her dressed that way before, but it suited the leader of the London vampire group.

"Justina," she greeted, tipping her head in greeting.

My boss was on her feet, shaking hands with them all.

The shapeshifter stepped back after he'd released Justina's hand, his gaze roaming over me. The cut of his suit showed his power, the strength of his jaw a contrast to his soft skin.

His oval eyes narrowed on my jacket. Did he know about the dagger? Why else would he be eyeing up my person?

"Nice to see you, Devon." Kalic spoke before anyone. "I see you've slotted in nicely here."

He was wearing a smile as well as jeans with a shirt. His outfit didn't match his wife's, which meant he wasn't playing her game.

"I have, thank you for noticing." What else could I say? We had crossed paths in the past, but we'd never formed a friendship. His wife on the other hand. "It's nice to see you, Antonia."

She grinned, throwing me a little wink when Justina stood. She knew we were there for business, not to catch up. And, yet, seeing her brought back a sad time in my life. She had held me in her basement with Kalic when the Dark Crawler was inside me. She had stopped them from killing me outright.

"This is Julian." Antonia introduced the man who stood next to her. "He's the leader of the shapeshifters. As you know, they've kept to themselves for centuries. Until recently."

Kurt indicated that our guests should take a seat. They accepted, sitting across from us and relaxing in their leather chairs. There was no threat, no underlining current. We were all there for the same reason. To keep our people safe.

"Latest I heard is that you've found where this fiend..." Antonia spat the word from her painted red lips. "...is hiding."

Leaning forward, Justina looked at each of them. She respected Kalic as much as she did Antonia. He might be her husband and not a leader, but he was the man who would always keep Antonia afloat. He was her rock. Someone she had relied on for hundreds of years. Would I ever find someone like that?

Glancing at Gerard, I wondered how the conversation with his sister had gone. He claimed that she had done well with her life, moving on despite her attack. So, why couldn't he?

"Yes. But, the place is heavily guarded. Not only by witch magic, but by vampires and shapeshifters." Justina's gaze roamed across both leaders. Their expressions were stoic, and yet, a tick in the jaw of Julian alerted me to his position. He had no idea.

"What do you mean?" And, neither did Antonia.

"We scoped out the place last night. Shapeshifters and vampires were on guard around the grounds of the estate. Do you know anything about this?" Gerard got to his feet, too on edge to stay seated for long.

"Of course we didn't. We would never allow our people to become involved with witch business. No offense." Kalic waved away my open mouth.

Yeah, it was best not to interfere with the politics between each group. Each coven, or band of supernaturals, had agreed to co-exist in peace. If that pact was broken, London city would become a hunting ground for those that would tear down its streets and kill the humans. The Dark Crawlers were already preying on humans too much as it was. However, the government was working on a way to eliminate them for good. That wasn't a fight I was interested in joining.

"Julian, I must admit, I don't know much about you or how your world works." Justina's expression was soft, her attitude welcoming.

The man wasn't exactly warm, his demeanour a little cool, although he wasn't a risk. He obviously wasn't used to being in such high esteemed company.

"I've been working more closely with Antonia since Kalic and I became friends. After some of my people went rogue, I needed to step out into London, just to show a little control." Straightening his royal blue tie, he looked at me. "I'm ready to work with the agency to make sure peace is kept in London. I can't have shapeshifters doing as they please. As you can imagine, they're powerful and... not very discreet."

What did Julian shift into? He looked like an exotic snake, especially when his tongue flicked out briefly. Wait, he wasn't watching me, he was looking at Kingsley as he slept on my shoulder.

"Please don't tell me you eat rats?" My raised eyebrows made him pause.

Throwing his head back, he howled with laughter.

Kalic and Antonia joined in, the hilarity spreading around the room. What had I said?

"No," Julian said through guffaws. "I'm not going to eat your familiar. I'm an eagle, yes, but every animal is my friend. I only eat when I'm in human form. I'm vegan."

It was my turn to laugh. The others joined in at the irony. Yes, it would make sense that he didn't eat animals, considering he was a leader of people who morphed into them.

"I applaud you," I muttered, wondering how he could resist a burger.

He shook his head as he grew serious again. "You wouldn't eat your familiar. It's a similar thing."

It was nice for someone to talk to me as if I was a witch. I'd felt so disconnected from both worlds, I'd forgotten how it felt to fit into one.

Smiling at him, I relaxed. He had good energy, which always warmed me to a person. I could feel it from across the room. He was open, honest. Something that hadn't been obvious straight away.

"You represent the witch world, we represent ours," Antonia said, glancing at Kalic. "What about the warlocks?"

Kurt held his hand in the air. "I've spoken to Maxwell Maddocks. He fully supports what we have to do. However, his people are the ones who are under threat. It's your people who are helping the culprit. Will you let us kill them?"

If my eyes could've popped out of my head, they would've. Kurt had just asked the leaders of two groups whether we could kill their people. Was he crazy? Or, had he taken some stupidity potion before he had entered the room? He might be amazing at herbology, but his brain cells were working against him.

Antonia's dark eyes connected with my gaze. I had been a little useless in keeping in contact, but we'd always shared a bond. A bit like Justina and I. We understood one another.

"The vampires that are helping the witch slave trade are traitors as far as I'm concerned. I trust Devon... and yourselves, of course, to take action the best way you see fit."

Leaning her elbows on her heavy wooden desk, Justina smiled gently at the vampire leader. "We won't automatically kill them. However, if we can't make them surrender, that may be the last case scenario."

My soul was vibrating with an unfamiliar feeling. Antonia had said that she trusted me before the others. That was a compliment. One that I promised to myself I would honour. The vampires would need to be punished, but the bloodshed had to be kept to a minimum.

Julian watched Justina, his gaze penetrating. And, yet, she stayed still, not backing down when he tried to intimidate her with his leadership power. She wasn't in a leadership role for a coven of witches, but she was the head of the Hunted Witch Agency. It was a well-deserved and respected position. She deserved the praise that everyone gave her. She got the job done, even if it took her years.

"I've worked on several cases in between this one. I have personal vested interest in capturing those that commit these atrocious crimes towards witches. I was kidnapped once too. My father was killed by the man who tried to drain my magic. But, I don't let it cloud my judgement. I have one goal only. To end the suffering of those that are being kidnapped. If I have your support, that end might be in sight."

Her head was held high as she spoke. The words were projected to everyone, but they hit Julian in the chest. His slight nod and narrowing of the eye told me more than any words. He saw that she meant what she said. She would find those responsible. It didn't really matter what he said. She had the government behind her, she would do what was needed.

"You have my permission to take down the shapeshifters involved in safeguarding those who have been committing these atrocities. By any means necessary."

Getting to his feet, Julian came over and extended his hand again. Justina took a deep breath as she got to her feet. Antonia came up behind her shapeshifter friend and put a hand on his shoulder. When she put her hand forward, it was face down. The others automatically realised that she was offering a show of solidarity. Their hands went on top to join in her gesture.

"It's agreed," Antonia said, her Eastern European accent strong. "We get these bitch witches and end this once and for all."

16

*I*t was time. Nothing was going to get in the way of capturing the most hunted witch in recent history. And, I was going to play a part in bringing her down. She must have been an Essex witch. My thoughts had been trying to process my family history and how she could be connected. How else would she have my mother's spells from her grimoire?

"Okay, guys, you're up in five. Hold tight." Justina's voice came through the walkie talkie.

They had dropped us off next to a back entrance. We were dressed in black to blend in with the night. Surveys of the castle had been sent over by the government. The short track we were hiding on was tucked away within the woodland surrounding the estate.

"I'm glad I wore the same colour as you," Maxwell said as we hid behind one of the high bushes.

Yes, for some crazy reason, Justina had allowed the leader of the warlocks to be a part of our mission. Apparently, he had vested interest. Considering the witch inside was trying to get enough power to wipe out the whole of the warlock race, I suppose I had to agree.

"Just make sure you keep an eye on us. We have the reflective strips on our jackets so the moon can show you where we are." Gerard zipped his jacket.

Mine was snug around my small frame, forcing me to have my dagger tucked into an outside pocket. Usually, I wouldn't mind, but today I'd put a lot of my warlock magic inside. It was starting to become a habit. One that I wasn't sure I wanted to continue.

"What did Becky say last night?" Gerard asked as we waited.

She had called me just as I was leaving the agency. Gerard had driven me home, listening to the conversation. I hadn't enlightened him when I came off the phone, too wrapped up in my own world to even say goodbye.

"She said that if I still wanted to give up my warlock magic, I would become a full Essex witch."

Maxwell's gasp resounded through the trees. Comforting somehow, considering we were about to raid the castle behind them.

"You'd be royalty. You could even start your own coven." Maxwell's tone was tight, apprehensive. Was that because of the potential of having me as a leader or because of the mission ahead?

A hand brushed my gloved fingers. Gerard. I knew just from the feel of his energy. He hadn't given me any of his magic today. I had been practicing my invisibility spells with my pure witch magic, so I would use them to my advantage tonight.

"He may have a good point. I'd be in your coven." His deep voice made me shudder.

"Oh, yeah, as co-leader, I take it?"

My cheeks heated when he grabbed my hand and squeezed. "It's nice to know you'd want mc by your side."

What? That wasn't what I had said. Not at all. He wasn't my... well, he'd have to be more than my work partner to lead a coven with me. And, at the rate we were going, that wasn't going to happen any time soon.

"Okay, go, go, go!" Justina's harsh whisper made us kick into gear.

Gerard led the way. We followed the sound of the crunch of his footsteps on the leaves and the small glow of the reflective strips on his jacket. Maxwell was behind me, his feet a little heavy on the ground for my liking. It didn't matter really, we were storming the place, not staking it out.

Justina, Kurt, and a whole team of experts were at the front entrance. Even more agents were at the two other entrances, leaving us with the hidden one.

Stepping onto the dirt track, right in front of the high wooden gates, Gerard paused. Maxwell moved forward, his arms extended out. Lifting my dagger, I stood beside him. Closing my eyes, I allowed the dark magic to filter up my body. My whole frame shook with the effort of holding so much at the same time as being connected to the earth's pure magic. If I let go of my witch magic, I would die. I knew that.

Maxwell formed a ball of pulsing dark blue energy. I held my magic inside my chest, waiting for him to be ready. My skin broke out in a sweat as my heart skipped beat after beat. My muscles started to strain from the tension. It had never been like this. I used to be able to handle it all, and now...

Arms came around my chest from behind. Gerard was supporting me, yet again. His witch magic filtered into me, giving me the power I needed to be confident to use my warlock magic.

"Okay," Maxwell said, his voice barely above a whisper. "Three, two, one..."

He thrust his ball forward, the large amount of magic exploding against the gates. They blasted apart as I unleashed my magic. Gerard let go as the heat of my body grew, probably searing him. The long line of red magic that came from my dagger cut a slice into the barrier spell.

"Let's go." Gerard was already moving towards the gate.

Dropping the power that surged through me, I followed behind Maxwell as he went through the gap after Gerard. My body was slow as I regained my breath, keeping my dagger ready for use.

The back of the castle had a small wooden door entrance. The courtyard was empty from any vehicle, apart from a motorbike. Ah, maybe Gerard would drive us out on it after our mission was complete. We could ride off into the London sunset.

"What are you doing?" The shout came from a vampire.

The only reason I knew it was a vampire was because his teeth was extended as he lunged towards me. My associates stopped in the middle of the yard as they were faced with several more of the cold skinned creatures.

Ducking, I rolled under the vampire, shoving my fist into his thigh. My blade sliced him to the bone as I pulled away, his cry followed by his body collapsing to the floor. Kicking his head to knock him out, I checked the others were okay.

"Get inside!" Gerard shouted as he punched a vampire in the jaw.

Maxwell was behind us, throwing balls of fire at our enemies. That was the perfect weapon. Pulling my own fireball into my hand, I cringed when my stomach cramped. Oh, dear, I'd used too much warlock power. My witch connection was thinning.

"Devon!" Maxwell shouted as another vampire appeared behind me.

Circling, I smiled and gave him a wink as I threw the ball straight at his chest. His howl was long, although he still moved. He surged forward, his arms wrapped around my legs as we went down, crashing to the hard ground.

He gripped my thighs, his head lowering with his sharp teeth exposed. Placing my hands on his shoulders, I screamed a fire spell. His whole body burst into flames. I scrambled out from under him, smacking my leggings where they'd caught fire. Holes appeared as the skin blistered. It was minor, nothing Kurt's herbs wouldn't fix.

"Fuck!" Gerard's shout was joined by a gurgling sound.

Spinning, I leapt across the yard to where he struggled with a vampire. It was hanging off his back, its head bend towards Gerard's neck. He was... No...!

Jumping up so I could reach him, I sunk the blade of my dagger up and under the vampire's ribs. He flinched, but he didn't let go of Gerard. I couldn't see my partner's face but his body started to sag, almost falling to the ground.

"Maxwell," I shouted. "Wood!"

A long sharp stick landed next to my feet. The warlock must have seen what was happening before I'd even reached the pair. Scooping it up from the ground, I ignored the grunt coming from the warlock leader and lunged at the vampire again, this time sinking the wood straight into his heart.

The body stilled and then burst into flames. Gerard collapsed on the ground as I patted his clothes to make sure he wasn't caught alight. He was silent, no words coming from his mouth. My heart hammered in my chest, almost breaking my ribs as I slowly turned him over.

"Maxwell!" The word was whispered on my breath.

Gerard's throat was almost ripped open. His eyes were closed, his breathing laboured. At least he was still alive. I could hear fighting behind me, but I couldn't bring myself to look away from my work partner. From the man who had become a part of my life. We weren't together, we weren't even in love, and yet... tears streamed down my face as I tugged off my jacket and tore the bottom of my T-shirt. Leaning over him, I placed my hand above the wound in his neck. Luckily, a soft light in the courtyard illuminated us, making it easier for me to see.

"I've got you covered," Maxwell called. "Help him."

Taking a shaky breath, I pulled on my witch magic. Whispering a healing spell, I tried to push the energy out of me, but I was too weak. The warlock magic that I'd used to rip through the barrier spell had taken it out of me.

"It's not working!" I shouted.

Shoving my jacket onto the wound, I tied it, ready to get him out of there. If I didn't get him to a hospital, or to Kurt, he would die.

Kurt!

The walkie talkie was on the ground. Maxwell huffed as he torched yet another vampire. It was actually the last one. No more seemed to be spilling from the open back doorway.

"Kurt, come in," I said into the receiver. "I need you!"

The crackle of the speaker made me want to throw the stupid thing. Gerard's lifeless body lay at my feet. His chest was rising and falling, slowly, calmly, almost peacefully.

"What's wrong?" Kurt's voice blasted from the talkie.

"You need to get to the back entrance. Gerard's been bitten by a vampire. He's not going to make it if you don't heal him!"

Maxwell joined me as I waited for the reply. My hands were shaking so badly, I almost dropped the walkie talkie. Bending down, the leader of the warlock checked over my poor handy work. I would never make a good nurse.

"I'm on my way, but you need to get inside, Devon. We have to carry on with the mission."

Nodding, I handed the device to Maxwell. However, my feet wouldn't allow me to move. They were stuck to the concrete. Falling to my knees, I sat beside Gerard, shaking him.

"Wake up!"

His eyes fluttered slightly, a sharp intake of breath making me seize his face in my hands. Looking into his gaze when his eyes opened slightly, I froze. His bright green irises were stunning. They pierced my soul as he stared.

"Devon," he somehow croaked. "Get inside-"

"No, I can't leave you." My whisper went ignored as he tried to move.

His cringe made my own neck hurt. He was in a lot of pain, and I couldn't help him. Why couldn't my magic heal him like Kurt's did?

"Listen to me," he whispered, his words taking all his energy. "This is the only chance we'll have to get her. Please... I know you can do it."

Tears dribbled down my face. I couldn't do it, I wasn't strong enough. I couldn't even get enough energy to cast a healing spell on him.

"Devon!" His voice grew stronger, angrier. "Stop doubting yourself!"

His hands grabbed my shoulders, tugging me down to him. His lips smashed against mine, his kiss hard, yet demanding. I thread my fingers through his hair, unable to pull away from the heady energy that intoxicated me.

The air left my lungs as he pushed me away, his body collapsing to the ground from lack of energy.

"Okay," I muttered, getting to my feet. "I'll get the bitch!"

He chuckled, his whole face screwing up in pain. "Go..."

Turning from him, I focused on my goal. The witch who had caused so much pain was inside. Gerard was willing to die for our cause, which meant I was too. No matter what happened, someone was going to die today.

And it wouldn't be any of us.

17

The corridors were empty, the guards too busy outside. That helped little old me immensely. Especially as I was currently creeping around the plush castle home, my dagger held out in front of me. I had left Gerard with Maxwell and the walkie talkie. The others wouldn't be able to keep track of me, but I had my phone if they really needed to. My mind wanted to go back to the kiss and the threat of Gerard's health. But, I couldn't dwell on it. I had a job to do.

Classical music played through speakers that came from the ceiling. It was eerie in an otherwise silent home. The walls were red, the lampshades black. It looked like I had stepped into the Moulin Rouge.

I wouldn't mind visiting Paris after all this was over. Maybe I could persuade Gerard to take me. He had kissed me, after all.

"Check on him!" The hurried whisper came from behind a door that wasn't quite closed. "The basement is the last place they'll look, but he's dangerous, he'll get them to help him."

The feminine voice was followed by a masculine grunt and heavy footsteps. Ducking behind a suit of armour, I waited. Touching the metal to check if it was real, I held my breath. Yes, it was a genuine medieval suit of armour. Bloody presumptuous arseholes.

"They're annihilating the security, we need to get out of here. The boss got out okay, so we need to save ourselves. I told her not to hire vampires or shapeshifters. They're useless!" The older man stormed from the room, a young girl in tow.

The pair rushed down the hall, towards the kitchen that I had just tiptoed through. My mission was to find the woman, but apparently she'd already escaped. Fuck. Crap. Fuck.

My footsteps were like a ballerina's as I retraced them back to the kitchen. I might as well find out who this man was. He might have some valuable information.

Hearing the sound of a clunky wooden door swinging open inside the kitchen, I slid past the open archway and hid against the wall. My breath was shallow and uneven as my nerves shook my insides. Why were they trusting me to find the bad guys? I was just a tiny little thing.

The buzz of magic that was ready to surge through the soles of my feet reminded me of who I was. Yes, I wasn't as powerful as I'd been just a year ago, but I could still wield both warlock and witch magic. Not only that... I was holding a dagger that I knew how to use. Sometimes, I just needed one thing. Faith. Faith and belief in myself. I could defeat the bad people. I was good enough. And, fuck me, if the Hunted Witch Agency trusted me enough to let me loose in a castle, I must be doing something right.

"Be careful," the man said as they disappeared.

Not waiting for the door to swing shut, I dove across the kitchen, the stone floor helping me slide faster. My arm only just managed to stop the door from clicking shut. Silently slinking into the darkness, I allowed it to close, the click hopefully reassuring those who had gone down the steps before me.

A tiny lightbulb lit the concrete steps that led to the basement. It was freezing, the cold stone pressing against my thin T-shirt. I had completely forgotten that I had taken my jacket off to try and stem Gerard's bloody neck.

"No, don't!" The feminine shout was followed by a scuffle.

My boots light on the stairs, I hurried down to the bottom. A scream rent the air as I rounded the corner and froze on the spot. The walls of the basement were ancient stone, the grey colour covered in wear and tear. There were several torture contraptions on the ground. Metal rings, with chains attached, hung from the hard stone surface of the walls. This wasn't a basement, it was a dungeon.

"Who are you?" A deep threatening voice came out from the shadows.

The man and woman who had come down before me were lying on the ground, their eyes staring up at the ceiling. Their expressions were contorted into fear, the blank look in their gaze a testament to the lack of life force in them.

249

Taking a deep breath, I pulled some warlock magic into my body. The whole room vibrated with energy, the kind that was always followed by power.

"I'm Devon..." I spoke to the darkness, unable to see past the tiny bulb above my head. "I'm with the Hunted Witch Agency. Are you...?"

I didn't know what to ask. He wasn't a witch. In fact, he was a warlock. I could feel his kinship with my own vibration as the shadows shifted. A tall thin man came out from behind an old upright iron chest. I hated to think what the owner did to the victims when they put them in there.

"Ah, Devon. I've heard a lot about you."

His dark hair was long and straggly, the ends scooped into a loose ponytail. He wore a tattered suit, the white shirt no longer its original colour. His eyes were small against a huge nose. He wasn't exactly a looker.

"What are you talking about?"

He knew my name. How was that possible? I had never seen the man in my life.

"You... you don't know?" He almost stumbled as he took a step closer.

Backing up, I raised my dagger, ready to ward him off. He might look harmless, but he had just killed two people. And, I had no idea how.

"Who are you?" My change of topic worked. For some reason, my instinct told me to keep him talking.

Often men liked to talk about themselves, especially warlocks. I wasn't one to judge or be sexist, but something about their magic made their heads swell with arrogance. I would use that to my advantage while I tried to suss him out. He was dangerous, that much I could tell.

"I'm Vernon Jupiter. You don't know me?" His surprise was in contrast to my blank expression.

Nope, I'd never heard of him. And from the look on his face, he was either constipated, or disgusted by that fact.

"I'm one of the most powerful warlocks in Britain. I'm the leader of the Stonehenge coven. Didn't your father teach you this? Considering his family line is at war with mine, I would've thought that his daughter would know."

Noticing a piece of dirt on the cuff of his sleeve, he stared at it, zoning out. He was my father's enemy? I had no idea about my father's family. What was it with all the ancestry lessons? Couldn't I just be a normal agent type woman? One who kicked arse and brought down the bastards who were giving the supernatural a bad name? No?

"She's been testing on me, you know," Vernon said, his eyes not quite able to focus. "That witch despises me."

"She does?" Ah, the perfect opportunity to find out more information about our person of interest.

Nodding, he leant against the death trap behind him. It looked like it would squash someone within seconds, the long iron spikes driving straight through the chest. Gruesome.

"Of course! I may have tricked her into falling in love with me. It was just a bit of fun." Waving his hand in the air, he almost fell over, only just getting his balance.

My hand was still extended, the blade pointing straight at him. It looked like he was drunk, but I knew better. The magic was making him crazy. That's what happened to warlocks when they were addicted.

"She's testing on you because you broke her heart?" Seriously? How cliché.

The muscles in my arm were straining, almost shaking. They were already sore from slaying the vampires. I wasn't sure how much longer I could keep it up.

His eyes narrowed on me, the irises flaring red in the dark. Oh, great, the bastard was hanging on by a thread.

"Do you know how much witch magic she's pumped into me?" He advanced, his footing stronger now. "I'll tell you... Three times a day. Yep," he almost screamed. "...three times a day she forces the magic she's drained from those witches into my skull. Just to torture me."

The shriek of his voice made me step back. If she had been filling him with all that magic, he would be too powerful for me to defeat. No matter how much magic I tried to use.

"She wants to destroy the warlocks," I said, keeping my gaze on him, but feeling behind me with my free hand. "We can't let that happen."

If I could get on his good side, maybe he would forget that he hated my father. Maybe. I didn't have much choice right now.

"No, we can't. I understand why she might want to do that. My coven didn't take too nicely to me messing around with a witch. They didn't just accept it like the London coven accepted your parents." A line of spittle left his wet lips as he threw his hand in the air.

A small puff of bright purple flames left his hand and smacked into the ceiling, causing dust to descend upon us.

Maybe my plan wasn't a good one. I'd reminded him that my father was a warlock who had got away with breaking the rules. Good one, Devon, bloody brilliant.

Coughing, I switched my dagger into the other hand to give me a break. Vernon, the crazy warlock, was still advancing. Actually, he was backing me into a corner. Moving to my right, I tried to get him to circle, but he wasn't interested. In fact, he froze, his eyes staring straight at me.

"You look just like her!" His cheeks blushed pink.

The silver of my dagger glinted in the overhead light. Ah, he could see me clearly now. And... who did I look like?

"Everyone keeps saying that. Who do I look like?" My anger got the better of me, my foot stamping on the hard ground.

"It seems you know nothing about your family, my girl. It's not surprising considering who they are. Disgusting lot of inbreds."

Gripping the handle of my dagger tighter in my palm, I controlled the urge to throw it.

It would be so simple to slaughter him, or attempt to, anyway.

"Don't talk about my family. Just tell me who the ring leader of the slave trade is, and I'll leave you alone." Not.

His grin was manic, the edges of his mouth stretching wide. I shuddered, unable to hold back my distaste any longer. He saw the movement, his gaze astute on me.

"How dare you screw your face up at me?! I'm powerful! I'm... going to kill you."

Before I could move, he threw a stream of red magic towards me. It wrapped around my legs, bringing me to my knees. I managed to keep my balance, my dagger still in hand. No, I couldn't let him get the better of me. I wasn't about to die by the hand of my father's enemy before I'd even found our target.

The ground was cold under my hands as I pushed myself into a stand, slicing the string of magic that bound me. "I don't think so."

Being arrogant, Vernon had been casually tucking his shirt in his waistline. He didn't have time to react when I threw the dagger. It plunged straight into his chest. On the right side.

Running towards him as he bent double, I jumped, my boots high in front of me. It was a good job I had been training between missions.

"Stop!" His hand extended and froze still.

And so did I.

My body shook as sweat broke out over my skin. I was hovering in mid-air, my legs thrown out in front of me. I couldn't move, couldn't put my feet down, or lift my arms. He could do anything to me. He could kill me. He could leave me stuck exactly like this. Somehow that would be worse than anything else he could do to me.

The skin on my arms suddenly flared hot as darkness crept into the corner of my eyes.

Vernon was wrenching my blade out of his chest with his spare hand. The other was still held high, obviously controlling the magic that froze me.

I couldn't have a panic attack. If I did, it would draw my focus away from the present. I needed to be in the present.

"Breathe as much as you want, I can still hear the racing of your heart, and the adrenaline running through your veins." Vernon studied my dagger, seemingly not affected by the gaping wound in his chest. His blood ran down the blade, coating his fingers. The man was magically insane.

Biting my tongue, I held back my retort. Diplomacy. Justina was always strict on diplomacy. As my deep breathing calmed my fight or flight reaction, I relaxed into the magic, allowing it to hold me.

Vernon touched the tip of the dagger, pressing it into his fingertip. There was no reaction on his face, no flinch, nothing. He was emotionally dead. Physically drained of any feeling.

"I think my coven will welcome me back with open arms when I deliver the body of Kevin Jinx's daughter." Slanting his head to the side, he stared at me. "An Essex witch's daughter. I heard you were struggling with your magic. I can help you with that. When you're dead, you won't even know."

My facial muscles struggled to move, but I managed to get my mouth open. "Why does your coven care about an Essex witch?"

It was good to encourage him to talk. The longer he didn't kill me, the more time the others had to find us before it was too late. Fingers crossed. If I could bloody well move them.

My dagger dropped to the ground when Vernon decided he was bored of it. The clatter of the metal made me jump, causing my body to jerk. Oh, that was interesting. Was the warlocks witch spell faltering?

Charging over to me, Vernon put his face close to mine. "Because you're the last one in your mother's line. You'll die without having a child. Meaning that the warlocks will have more claim to the earth's power."

"You will?"

Huh? Someone really needed to give me a proper history lesson. And soon.

The sneer aimed at me was accompanied by bad breath. Ew. And, I couldn't even move my head out of the way. Yuck.

"Well, yes, young lady. The earth's pure magic is controlled by the head of the Essex witches. Didn't you know that? Why do you think the people of Salem in America allowed your kind to go over there? Although, unfortunately for us, you managed to stay hidden here." His scoff of disgust made me hold my nose closed so I didn't have to smell his stale breath.

Flicking his wrist, he suddenly released me. My body flew forwards, my legs crashing straight into the iron chamber. My boots were sturdy, but the impact buckled my ankles, the pain wrenching up my legs.

"It feels good to be talking to a warlock after all these witches. Although..." He spun on one of his worn out loafers. "...you're not exactly pure... even if you can use their magic. Look at me... I'm doing the same."

Crawling up to my feet, I clenched my teeth as I tested my weight on my legs. Nothing was broken. Bonus.

"You won't last. The magic will kill you. Trust me, I know." My voice was low, unobtrusive.

The shake of my hand was hidden as I tucked it behind my back. Drawing on the magic that seemed to come easier to me, I let it sit in my chest as I waited for him to reply.

Rolling his neck, he laughed when the bones cracked, causing me to wince. I hated it when people did that. It grossed me out.

"Okay, enough chit chat. Your father killed mine in their dispute. My family line has tried to tap into the magic that the Essex witches control, but we've been stopped at every turn. Not anymore."

Lifting both hands, Vernon started to hum. A swirling egg of light appeared, black lines threading through the magic. It was darkness mixed with light. Great, I could handle it. Couldn't I?

Diving for my dagger as he tossed the ball towards me, I crashed into the stone wall.

My head buzzed from the impact and unspent energy, ready to leave me.

"You won't win this one. You're not powerful enough." His chuckle echoed around the room as he formed an arrow of fire and launched it in my direction.

"Yes, she is!" The shouted words vibrated in my head so hard, I had to clasp it.

What the...?

Two shadows moved into the room. My eyes were squinting from the pain. Someone was casting a spell too powerful for me to fight back. Was it Justina? Kurt?

"Devon?"

My stomach flipped, butterflies dancing as sweat sprouted across my whole body. No, it couldn't be.

Blinking, I tried to focus on the approaching figure. Throwing my arms out when they reached me, I tried to bat them away. It was a cruel trick. A very sick trick.

"Devon, don't resist the magic. Allow it." The deeper voice made me glance to my right.

Relaxing, I released my clenched muscles. The pain in my head slunk away, leaving a warm glow filtering through me.

"You will not defeat me!" The scream of Vernon as he swirled his arm made me stare.

A tornado of wind, multi-coloured magic and fire made me back up against the cold stone wall. There was no way we could put him down.

"Darling..." The woman who stood to my left spoke as she grabbed my hand. "...work with us."

"Mum?" I croaked, my voice cracking.

How were my parents there? They couldn't be. They were dead. Weren't they?

The woman who had taught me to be a witch shook me, bringing me back to the present. Her brown eyes contrasted against her fair skin as the wind wiped her dark hair around her head.

"We can beat him!"

Yes, we could. I could. They could. If we worked together, our magic just might be enough to bring him down.

Glancing at my father as he moved closer to the ever growing swirl, I tried to hold my emotions in check. He wasn't exactly tall, but his broad shoulders were familiar to me. I had sat on them plenty of times when I was young.

"Mum," I said, taking her arm when she tried to drag me forward. "I'm too weak. I... it's hard to explain."

She shook her head as she looked into my eyes. "I know all about your magic."

Holding up my dagger, I smiled. "So, you know about this, too?"

Her eyebrows lowered. No, apparently not. Okay, that was a good thing. Maybe she would trust me to do what I needed to do.

"You need to go with dad. Weaken Vernon. I'll do the rest."

Her nod made me straighten my spine. She didn't question whether I could do it. In fact, she took my word for it. That was crazy. She shouldn't trust me, I wouldn't.

Planting my feet firmly on the ground, I held the handle of my dagger with both hands. The blade pointed downwards as I tried something new. The air around me intensified as Vernon's crazy assault started to expand. He stood, his head thrown back and his arms spread wide. He had completely lost it.

"Okay," I whispered, suddenly wishing Kingsley and Gerard were there to support me. "Come on mother earth."

Closing my eyes, I shut out the chanting of my mum. Her Essex powers would probably lend us a lot more magic than I'd realised.

Concentrating on the earth beneath my feet, I bent down and placed the tip of the dagger against the hard ground. A zap of energy flung into the silver, making me gasp. Yes, I could do it.

Instead of drawing the magic up through my body, I would bring my warlock power straight into the blade. That way, it couldn't strip me of my witch magic.

Opening my eyes when my hands jerked, I bit back a smile. I'd done it. The whole dagger was covered in yellow flames. I was ready.

"Let's do this."

Standing stock still, I held up the dagger and got ready to throw. My mother was on Vernon's left, and my father on his right. A stream of white magic spurted from my dad's hand. What the...? It went straight into Vernon's chest, sinking into his skin.

My mother then flicked her wrist, sending the funnel of magic flying into its owner. Vernon crashed against the wall, the force of his own magic pinning him. Now, it was my turn.

My arm muscles tensed as I flung the dagger towards my target. Vernon laughed as he brought his head forward and stared at me. The dagger stopped just before it hit his face. No!

"Kevin Jinx, your daughter is someone to be reckoned with. But, I'll still kill her."

My boots thumped against the floor as I ran straight for the warlock. The shock on my mother's face made me grin. She looked impressed. And, so she should be. I was Devon Jinx. Half witch, half warlock.

"Careful!" My father shouted as the dagger flipped.

The wind was strong, my body slow. It felt like I was moving through mud, and yet, I pushed through. He would not win. I still had too much to do.

Dodging to the side, I watched as my dagger flew into the stone wall. And dug itself deep. Hum. Maybe I should've listened to Gerard when he suggested I lift weights.

"Devon, go!" My mother shouted.

They were still using Vernon's magic against him. His whole body was shuddering against the wall on the opposite side of the room, but his fingers were working loose. Once he was free, we were all dead.

"Thanks, Mum!"

It took me three leaps as I almost ran straight into the wall. My fingers wrapped around the handle of the dagger, the magic in it almost burning my palm. Oh, my power was good. Almost too good.

"Duck!" I shouted as I wrenched the loosened blade from the wall.

Spinning, I launched the dagger to my left, hoping the momentum would bring it round full circle. My father dropped to the floor as the funnel of wind snatched the blade, sending it slicing straight through Vernon's neck, the flames exploding in his face.

My mother ducked as it carried on, smacking straight into the stone beside my head. Shit, that was close.

As the magic in the room dropped, so did I. My knees couldn't hold me any longer. I had used all of my magic and borrowed some too.

"Devon," my mother called, coming straight over. "You did it!"

They were by my side, holding me, crying against me. I let the tears stream from my face as the two people who had brought me into the world held me against them. My heart exploded in my chest as my world crumpled around me.

"Is everyone okay?" Kurt's bellow made us pull apart.

He thundered into the room, followed by Justina. I gripped my father as he lugged me to my feet. Gerard...

"Is she okay?" His deep voice was weak, but it was there.

He came into the room, supported by Maxwell. The others were checking that Vernon was dead. Which he was. Thanks to me.

The corner of Gerard's lip lifted into his cheek when he spotted me. He heaved a sigh of relief and then promptly sat on the bottom step of the stairs he'd just negotiated. He had literally come to check on me.

"Well done," Kurt said coming over. "Who are you?"

Laughter bubbled in my chest as my parents frowned, obviously affronted by Kurt's blunt manner.

"These are my parents," I introduced them, grinning like an idiot.

My chest swelled as I looked around at my team. They were covered in blood as they surveyed the area, making sure we were safe. Gerard watched me, pain etched into his features. A small smile danced on his lips. He was happy. Which made me happy.

Justina came over, her hands planted firmly on her hips. Okay, her composure wasn't as welcoming as I'd expected. In fact, Kurt's gaze also narrowed on the people I had lost.

"What's going on?"

Reaching unconsciously for my mum when Justina bit the inside of her cheek, I almost blocked my ears. For some reason, I knew that whatever she was about to say wasn't going to make me jump for joy. Or, even for shit. Nope, it was going to be much, much worse.

"Devon, I think your parents forgot to mention one very important detail." Justina's glare was lethal. Shit, it was bad.

"What's that?" My question was tentative, almost inaudible.

Releasing her breath, Justina crossed her arms over her waist, her ire aimed directly at my parents. "They failed to tell you that your grandmother is the one who's kidnapping the witches. She's the leader of the witch slave trade."

Other Series by Rachel Medhurst

Avoidables

The Deadliners Trilogy

Viking Soul Series

Zodiac Twin Flame Series

Author

Rachel Medhurst grew up in Surrey, England. She writes to prove that no matter where you come from, you can be anything you want to be. Your past may shape you, but it doesn't define you. When Rachel isn't writing, she can be found reading and walking in nature.

Printed in Great Britain
by Amazon